CW00547887

TEA IS FOR TROUBLE

A HAUNTED TEAROOM COZY MYSTERY

KAREN SUE WALKER

LARAGRAY PRESS

Copyright © 2021 by Karen Sue Walker

All rights reserved.

Published by Laragray Press

No part of this book may be reproduced in any form or by any electronic or mechanical means without written permission from the author, except for the use of brief quotations in a book review.

This is a work of fiction. All names, characters, locales, and incidents are products of the author's imagination and any resemblance to actual people, places, or events is coincidental.

Note from the Publisher: The recipes contained in this book have been tested, and to our knowledge are correct if followed exactly as written. Cooking and baking are subject to variables outside of our control; we are not responsible for results due to errors or typos in the ingredients or instructions. The publisher and author are not responsible for any adverse reactions to the recipes contained in this book.

Note from Author: I've done my very best to make sure these recipes are accurate and will provide great results, but I must admit that I am not perfect (no matter how hard I try!)

For more information about me and all my books or to contact me, visit http://karensuewalker.com.

ACKNOWLEDGEMENTS

My gorgeous cover was designed by Mariah Sinclair, the bestest cozy cover designer in the universe. You can find her at https://www.thecovervault.com or on Facebook.

More grateful thanks to my critique group members—you've made me such a better writer: Sherry, Leslie, Lisa, Dianne, Michaele, and Jill. And to my original critique partner Diana —your support and friendship has meant the world to me.

The support and encouragement of the Southern California Writers Association (https://www.southerncalwriters.org) is priceless. Thanks to Maddie, Larry, Diana (again) and all the wonderful writers in this now nationwide group. If you're a writer or aspiring writer, join us for virtual fun, networking, and great learning opportunities.

Thanks to the Ukulele Granny, Linda, for your proofreading expertise.

Finally, most of all to my readers. You give me inspiration, ideas, moral support, and encouragement (and find the most persistent of typos!). You are what makes all the hard work worthwhile.

DEDICATION

To my 1667 Club friends

You're a wonderful, wacky, and generous bunch of authors, and I don't know how I ever would have gotten through the past year without you and all the laughs! Anne, Rose, Martina, Shari, Lucinda, Elise, Lynda, Heather, Jenna, Brena, Mary, and Beverly. Love you guys!

CHAPTER 1

*T*he road to your dreams can be bumpy. It can also be covered in nails, which is how I ended up with two flat tires in the northern California town of Serenity Cove, population 963.

I heard a clunk at the same time the car lurched to the right. By the time I found a place to pull over, two tires had been reduced to shreds. I perked up at the sight of an auto shop, then deflated at the closed sign. I could have called roadside assistance, but Serenity Cove seemed like as good a place as any to stop and figure out the rest of my life. I wrote a note for the mechanic and shoved it, along with my keys, through the door.

Checking my phone for nearby lodging, I found two choices, a chain hotel and the Serenity Cove Bed and Breakfast. I headed toward the B&B, rolling my suitcase behind me past cottages, mid-century mansions, and Victorian homes.

Soon I heard the ocean's thrum and breathed in the salty air. I turned the corner and stopped in awe of the untamed sea, its waves crashing violently against the rocks, sending spray high into the air. Its power and passion took my breath away.

Mesmerized, I headed for the water, found a boulder to perch on, and watched the pounding surf. The tension of the past few weeks slipped away, and the reality of a life alone sunk in. A little crab lay on its back, its legs flailing as it tried to upright itself.

"Hi, little guy. I'll help you." I stepped onto the wet sand, intending to flip it over, but a wave crashed over it before I got to it. When the wave retreated, it scurried back to the sea.

I'd been floundering like that little crab for so long waiting for someone to come along and fix everything. Like a wave, the heartbreak of losing my mother had righted me, and now it was time to learn to stand on my own two feet. At least I had the luxury of starting over at the age of forty-nine. Not all women had that chance.

Wiping a single tear from my cheek, I stood to resume my search for the B&B. I turned around and gasped. Across the street stood an enormous purple and pink Victorian house, majestic and absurd in its beauty and impracticality. It stood tall and wide, anchored to the ground as it must have been for a century.

I felt a strong pang of envy for whoever lived there. I envisioned a family--two parents and two or three children, all dressed in clean, freshly ironed clothes. No doubt those children always had milk for their cereal.

My envy evaporated. A sign said FOR SALE in foot-tall letters, and underneath, Perrino Realty and a phone number.

I dialed the number.

"Serenity Cove Real Estate," the voice said. "Harold Perrino speaking."

"How soon can you be here to show me the Victorian on Ocean View Drive?"

"Which Victorian?"

I sighed. How many Victorians did he have for sale? I gave him the address while I looked up the listing on my phone to check the price.

"Is the sign up already?" he asked. "It's not supposed to go up yet."

"But the house is for sale. I just looked it up online." I tried to keep the impatience out of my voice. "I'd like to see it this morning."

He hesitated. "I see. I don't know if I can make it today. How about tomorrow? Will your husband be joining us?"

"No." I thought of all the things I might tell this chauvinistic jerk, but I wanted to see the house. "I'll wait at the house for you, and if you don't come within the hour, I'll call another agent." With that, I disconnected.

I heard a chuckle behind me and spun around. A tiny woman in huge, red-framed glasses and short, spiky silver hair, tapped a gnarled walking stick on the ground. As she came closer, I guessed her to be at least seventy, but a vibrant, spry seventy.

"What's so funny?" I asked.

"Harold is the only agent in town." She poked her stick at the hedges as if trying to root out vermin.

"Then I'll get someone from another town."

She nodded knowingly. "Do you plan to turn it into a library? We could use one."

"A library?" I glanced at the house again, wondering if it had been a library at one time. "Why would you think that?"

"My mistake," she said, not appearing the least bit contrite. "I thought you were a librarian." She gestured at my clothes. "Monochromatic color scheme, sensible shoes, hair in a ponytail. I bet you're a big fan of the Oxford comma."

This conversation had taken an unexpected turn. "What does the Oxford comma have to do with anything?"

I couldn't tell if her smile was friendly or condescending.

We stared each other down until she finally said, "Would you like to see inside or not?"

She poked her walking stick at the shrubbery until she unearthed a key. As she opened the front door, she introduced herself as Irma Vargas, owner of the Mermaid Cafe.

"I'm April May." I waited for the inevitable questions that always came, but she didn't acknowledge my unique name. Following her into the house, I expected a small entryway or foyer as I'd seen in other Victorian homes, but instead I stood in a cavernous room with ceilings twelve or thirteen feet high. Thick layers of ivory paint obscured the grooves of the wainscoting, while faded floral wallpaper reached from the chair rail to the crown molding. Pale blue and cream-colored square tiles covered the floor in a diamond pattern.

"Do you know why there are two front doors?" My voice echoed in the nearly empty room.

"The home was designed for two families. This would have originally been the reception area for the lower residence. While that area," she pointed toward the other door, "was the entryway for upstairs."

Between the two doors, a huge bay window provided a stunning view of the ocean. A café table sat nearby, flanked by two upholstered chairs, and I imagined curling up in one with a cup of tea and a plate of scones and clotted cream.

Irma showed me where the walls had originally stood, and explained that because of the home's design, each floor had its own kitchen. "Augustus Thornly had the house built for his two daughters, Norma and Barbara. He hoped they would spend their lives here, each marrying and raising their family under the same roof. Rather naïve, if you ask me."

"Who took all the walls out? And why?"

"When Barbara got married and moved away, Norma turned the first floor into a French restaurant. It stayed open for several decades until she passed away. Barbara moved back in and took it over, but it wasn't the same. The restaurant closed back in the nineties, and she spent most of her time on the upper floor. Thank goodness her estate didn't decide to turn the place into a cat house."

"Excuse me?" I wasn't sure I'd heard her right.

"She left everything to a cat rescue group."

The moment I heard her words, I envisioned cats running around the room and up and down the staircase. I silently laughed at their antics, and then my vision morphed into a tearoom full of tables set with fine china and tiered trays.

I could open a tearoom and live on the second floor. It had been my mother's dream, our dream, once upon a time. On road trips, she pointed out houses, saying, "That would make a nice tearoom, don't you think?" or "Wouldn't this be a nice town to open our tearoom?"

Irma gestured toward the back of the house. "The kitchen is through there."

My mouth dropped open when I stepped through the door. A stainless steel six-burner stove with a griddle and two ovens took up half of one wall along with a huge sink. A brass and stainless cappuccino machine sparkled in the corner. I pictured myself drinking lattes while I rolled out dough on the island in the center of the room.

A sudden chill made me shiver. Once the appliances were up and running and the ovens were in use baking scones and other treats, it would be toasty warm, but right now I had goose bumps up and down my arms.

"Is this supposed to be the refrigerator?" I opened an office sized fridge built into a lower cabinet. A restaurant or even a tearoom would need plenty of refrigerator space.

Irma pointed her stick at the back door. "Through there. Norma expanded the mudroom."

I stepped through the back door into a spacious storeroom. Wire shelves on one side held crockery, pots and pans, and various utensils.

"Wow." Two tall cabinets would hold enough non-perishables to last for months. I opened the refrigerator, and although it smelled musty, it would be fine after a quick cleaning with baking soda. Toward the back of the room stood a walk-in freezer. I tried the door, but it didn't budge. A washer and dryer took up the opposite space to the right of the back door.

I peered through the window at the back yard where lush, green grass stretched to the back fence. The yard appeared sizable enough for small, summer events like bridal or baby showers. A wooden one-car garage painted to match the house sat in the back corner of the lot.

I followed Irma up a flight of stairs covered in a thick, floral runner. The second-floor layout mimicked the downstairs with the walls still intact. One bedroom sat empty, while the other two were tastefully furnished in an out-of-date yet charming style, with chintz comforters and lace-trimmed curtains.

We returned to the main floor, where Irma explained, "You could easily turn the place back into two residences, and you could rent out the upper floor. Or keep it for a guest suite when family comes to visit."

I shook my head. "It's absolutely perfect the way it is. I'm going to open a tearoom."

Her mouth dropped open, but before she could reply, a dapper, gray-haired man in a dark suit walked through the door.

"Harold, how nice you could make it." She smiled at him, but I sensed tension. "This lady wanted to see the house, and I understood you were too busy to show it." They stared at each other, barely hiding their hostility. She turned to me. "This is Harold Perrino, our local real estate agent."

"April May." I reached my hand to shake his.

"April May, what a unique name." He smiled, his dazzling blue eyes crinkling at the corners, momentarily distracting me. He told me a few details about the house and explained that the trust preferred to sell the house as-is, including the furnishings.

"That will be fine," I said. "I'm prepared to offer full price."

"I see." He swallowed hard. "Well…"

"Is there a problem?"

"Actually, yes, there is. You see, there's another offer on the house."

"Is it a full price offer?"

"Yes." His smile no longer reached his eyes.

I could spot a lie from twenty feet. Perhaps he thought another offer would be a good negotiating tactic. "I'm offering full price in cash. Please contact the seller and let them know. I assume you are prepared to write up the offer now?"

His smile had disappeared, and beads of sweat appeared on his forehead. "Yes, of course."

"There's more." I ignored his raised eyebrows. "I'm prepared to wire the funds, and I'd like to rent the house until escrow closes. I'd like to move in tomorrow."

Harold and Irma both seemed taken aback. "Tomorrow?" they said in unison.

I gave Harold a reassuring smile. "If I may have your card, I'll meet you at your office this afternoon to sign whatever additional paperwork you need. If you would text me the banking information, I'll arrange the wire transfer."

Harold pasted on a grin and handed me his card. "I'll speak to the owners, but you do realize it's Sunday."

"Do your best and give me a call or text." I gave him my cell phone number. "I'm staying at the B&B."

A soft howl came from above, perhaps the second floor or the attic.

I gazed up at the ceiling. "What was that?"

"What was what?" Irma asked.

"That sound."

Irma's blank expression gave me the impression she hadn't heard a thing.

"These old houses," Harold said. "They make all kinds of strange noises. You'll get used to it."

CHAPTER 2

*T*he innkeeper at the Serenity Cove Bed and Breakfast, a thin man whose clothes hung limply on his frame, allowed me to check in early.

"What time is breakfast tomorrow?" I asked.

"Seven till ten."

"What do you serve?"

"That depends."

"Depends on what?"

He handed me a room key. "Depends on what my wife decides to cook."

I climbed the carpeted stairs to a cramped but comfortable room decorated in shades of pink from the rugs to the wallpaper to the curtains. I could live with it for one night.

On the nightstand, I found a three-ring binder with the amenities of the B&B and the town. On a page titled "Dining" I found only three entries: The hotel dining room, Irma's restaurant--the Mermaid Café, and Tony's Pizza.

Not being a huge fan of chain hotels or pizza, I went downstairs and asked the innkeeper for the directions to the Mermaid Cafe.

"Walk to the ocean and turn left," he said.

"And?" I prompted.

"It's at the pier."

Thankful I didn't have to try to make small talk with the man, I made it halfway to the front door when he cleared his throat.

"Opens at four p.m.," he said.

Not wanting to wait three hours to eat, I asked what other choices I had for lunch.

"Hotel or Tony's Pizza."

"Yes, I saw that in the information you left in my room. Very helpful. What other choices might there be?" I told myself to be patient. Small towns moved at a slow pace, and I'd need to get used to it if I planned to move here.

"Well." He paused, and I waited for him to continue, tapping my foot impatiently. "Grocery has a deli. Sandwiches aren't bad."

"And where is the grocery store?"

"'Bout two miles north."

A deli sandwich didn't seem enough motivation to take a four-mile round-trip walk, so I called Tony's and put in an order for delivery. I ate the greasy pepperoni pizza in the parlor area, offering the laconic innkeeper a slice. He politely declined.

My phone buzzed with a text from Harold, saying the board of the cat rescue who owned the house wouldn't be available to meet to go over my offer until the next day.

I brushed away my disappointment and spent the afternoon researching permits and licenses required to open my tearoom. The list seemed enormous and daunting. "Take things one step at a time, April," I told myself.

Shortly after five o'clock, I headed for the Mermaid Café for dinner, following a path along the beach. I spotted the hotel through the gray mist a mile or two past the pier. The ten-story, nondescript building didn't appear enticing, but no doubt its dining room would offer an adequate menu if the Mermaid Café didn't pan out.

I soon reached the ramshackle, little pier where a few determined fishermen remained. Seagulls circled overhead, squawking loudly. A fishy odor filled my nostrils, combined with the smell of seaweed and the smell of something cooking. A small wooden building clung to the cliff next to the pier. Nets with starfish decorated the weather-worn exterior along with signs, "Open at 4PM" and "No shirt, no shoes, no service."

Not especially impressed by the exterior, I peeked through a porthole window. My second thoughts evaporated as I peered into the magical room. I stepped into the dimly lit interior, which glowed in shades of aqua and lilac reflected against textured silver walls mimicking undulating underwater waves.

Above me, light filtered down from behind frosted-glass turtle shells. A see-through bar, filled with sand and seashells, stretched along the left side of the room. Along the right, five plush booths nestled against the wall.

Patrons filled the booths, drinking martinis and speaking in civilized tones. In contrast, the men at the bar wouldn't have looked out of place on a chain gang.

Feeling awkward with several pairs of eyes on me, I took a seat at a table at the back by the floor-to-ceiling windows providing a breathtaking view of the ocean. Waves rhythmically churned and crashed on the beach below, while the sun, low in the sky, glittered on the water. A woman with long pink and blue hair headed my way.

As she approached, I realized the woman was Irma attired in a wig and a shell bra on top of a flesh-colored leotard. A sparkly apron wrapped around her waist completed the look, which might have been more appropriate on a woman half her age.

She greeted me with, "Well, look what the cat drug in." I heard soft chuckles coming from the bar. "I hope you changed your mind about the old Thornly place."

"Nope. I made an offer on it."

She nodded, then pulled out a chair and sat across from me. She gave me a sly grin. "Now that I've insulted you, hopefully they'll quit staring."

"What do you do when tourists come into town? Do you insult them too?"

She snorted. "We're on our best behavior for three or four months. You can't expect us to pretend to be friendly year 'round. You do know tourism is a seasonal industry, right?"

"Of course," I lied. I knew nothing about the hospitality industry. I hadn't even made a business plan. But I wasn't about to admit that. "When I open, people will come from San Francisco, the Bay Area, Silicon Valley..."

"Is that so? They're going to drive two hours for tea?" The way she said it told me she had her doubts, but that didn't bother me. I'd prove to everyone I could make Thornly House into something special.

I jumped at the sound of someone clearing his throat behind me and turned to see a man with weathered skin and a shaggy gray beard.

"Did I hear you're re-opening the restaurant?" His gruff voice barked out the words. "That'll be good news. No place to eat but this dump."

"I'm opening a tearoom." I guessed this man wouldn't know a scone from a dinner roll.

"Tea? No food?" He jerked his head back. "No one drinks tea around here."

He waddled back to the bar where his drinking buddy

slapped him on the back as if he'd done something noble by confronting me.

Irma handed me a menu, and as I glanced at the limited selection of entrees—steak, chicken, or seafood—she told me about the special. Cioppino. I ordered the special and a glass of white wine.

I'd finished half my glass of wine when Irma placed a steaming, fragrant bowl in front of me. Clams, mussels, and shrimp swam in a garlic-tomato broth. One sip told me I would return to the Mermaid Cafe regularly.

After a walk along the ocean back to the B&B, I went up to my room, changed into pajamas, and climbed into bed with my laptop. Pulling the fluffy comforter around me, I searched for websites of tearooms around the world for inspiration and ideas. Then I began learning more about the types and varieties of teas and how best to brew them. I'd learned a lot from my mother, but there was plenty more to discover.

At midnight, I shut the laptop and turned off the light. With my head on the pillow, I waited for sleep to come. My body ached with exhaustion, but my mind wouldn't slow down enough for me to fall asleep. Was I making a mistake? I'd made impulsive decisions before, and they'd always worked out fine. Better than fine.

After an hour of tossing and turning, I dressed and tiptoed down the stairs, hoping not to wake my hosts or other guests. A walk might help clear my mind of all my jumbled thoughts.

Without planning it, I headed straight for the ocean, and turned left, following the path along the water. Soon, I found myself across the street from my new home. The same enchantment came over me as it did when I'd first laid eyes on it. I already thought of it as my home. I'd lost count of the number of times I'd moved, both as a child and an adult, and I looked forward to settling down.

A light flickered from inside the second story. Had someone forgotten to turn out a lamp? Or—heaven forbid—left a candle burning? I watched the light disappear then reappear in the attic. Someone was in my house.

CHAPTER 3

*H*arold sounded grumpy on the phone about being woken up. I asked him who might be in the house, and whether I should call the police, but he told me to stay put, and he would be right over. I waited in the chilly night for him to arrive, pulling the hood of my jacket over my head when it started to drizzle.

Ten minutes later, his car pulled up on the street next to me. "Wait here," he said, and I waited while he crossed the street and entered the house. I hoped I hadn't sent him into a dangerous situation, but he was the one who didn't want to call the police.

Within minutes, the lights on the main floor came on, and curiosity got the better of me. Stepping through the front door, I found Harold talking to a middle-aged man with gray, straggly hair.

The man stopped speaking and turned to glare at me. "Are you the one who's stealing my home from me?"

"Excuse me?"

"I'm the rightful owner," he claimed. "This was my mother's house, and my aunt had no right to leave it to someone else."

His accusation made no sense to me, and I wondered if his claim carried any weight.

"This is Bob Shimp," Harold explained. "His mother owned the house before she passed away."

Perhaps the man's grief had led to confusion about his mother's intentions. "I'm sorry for your loss, but your mother left the house to the cat rescue, and they've sold it to me."

"That was my aunt," Bob said. "My mother died in 1989, and Aunt Barbara moved in. She'd just lost her husband. I wasn't about to throw her out on the streets, was I?"

I figure it was a rhetorical question, so I merely nodded.

"When she passed away, I find out she's cut me out of the will. She can't do that. At the very least, half of the house should go to me. My mother didn't leave her half to her sister instead of me. She wouldn't do that."

Harold patted Bob on the shoulder. "But, Bob, without proof--"

"I have proof. I have a copy of my mother's will. And I'm seeing a lawyer tomorrow to keep this sale from going through." He turned to me. "You won't get away with this." He pushed past me toward the front door.

I bristled at his accusation, and I let my anger get the better of me. "Hey, Bob," I called out as he left. "Just stay out of the house until you have a legal right to enter."

"I'll talk to him," Harold said, and followed him out the door.

Once outside, I searched through the rose bushes until I found the hidden key. Pocketing it, I headed back to the B&B.

∽

My phone alarm jerked me out of a deep sleep, and for a moment I didn't recognize the room. After decades of living out of a suitcase, I was accustomed to spending my first few moments of wakefulness in a confused state. I heard the surf faintly in the distance and it all came back to me.

"Serenity Cove," I whispered. I felt a thrill of excitement and nervousness remembering the previous day's events, smiling as I pictured myself bustling about in my tearoom serving sandwiches and scones to my patrons.

Pale light filtered through the sheer white curtains giving the pink room a grayish cast. I threw the comforter aside and slipped into my slippers, shuffling to the window. Outside, a thick bank of fog obscured the view, giving the scene a mysterious quality.

Soon dressed and eager for the day to begin, I made my way downstairs to the parlor where enormous muffins shared a sideboard with fruit and bagels. But first, I needed caffeine. I didn't see any teabags or hot water, so I made a beeline for the coffee. Picking out a mug that said, "Don't go bacon my heart," I filled it with coffee and a dash of creamer. The blueberry muffins looked delicious, so I grabbed one and found a seat at one of the round wooden tables decorated with a vase of pink roses.

A plump, forty-ish woman emerged from the kitchen wearing a ruffled pink apron and a wide smile. "Good morning, Miss May. I trust you slept well?"

"Please call me April."

"April May," she said with a smile. "What a lovely name. I'm Sarah. The muffins just came out of the oven, so they should still be warm. I love it when the butter melts into all the nooks and crannies, don't you? I see you picked blueberry. I made carrot, too. Feel free to have one of each or take one for later. I hope my husband took good care of you when you checked in."

"Yes, of course." I found Sarah's chattiness a welcome contrast to her husband's taciturn manner. "I'll be staying another night after all."

She grinned and clapped her hands together. "I'd hoped you would. We don't get many visitors this time of year. I like having the company. That's why we decided to open a B&B. I love meeting new people."

"You have a lovely place," I assured her. "I'm hoping to hear from the mechanic soon to tell me my car's ready."

Did I imagine a snicker? "Yes, of course. But you should know we move slower here than in the big city. I like it that way, though sometimes I do get a little impatient. You're from Sacramento, aren't you?"

"You could say that." A few months earlier, I'd given up my apartment and moved my meager belongings into my mother's home temporarily. I'd planned to move into my fiancé's home in Menlo Park after the wedding.

Sarah fixed herself a cup of coffee and returned to my table. "I'm all caught up on my morning chores. May I join you?" She reached for the chair across from me.

I nodded. "I'm waiting to hear from the real estate agent."

Her brown eyes widened. "So, it's true. I didn't believe it when I heard. You're buying Thornly House?"

"Yes." I smiled. "I'm going to open a tearoom and live in the upstairs quarters."

"Lovely." Her smile faded.

"Okay, what's wrong?" I could always tell when people's words didn't match their feelings, but it didn't take a mind reader to know she wasn't telling me something. "Does the house have termites?"

"No, nothing like that." She didn't make eye contact with me. "It's just…"

I waited for her to finish her sentence. All my years in sales taught me you could learn a lot if you could tolerate an uncomfortable silence. The other person would eventually fill it, often providing the information you wanted, and someone as chatty as Sarah couldn't help spilling the beans.

"Well, you see…" Sarah hesitated.

"Yes?" I prompted.

"There's a ghost."

CHAPTER 4

I laughed. That was the last thing I expected her to say "You're telling me Thornly House is haunted?"

She grimaced. "You may think it's ridiculous, but you don't have to laugh at me."

Her serious tone caught me off guard. I hadn't meant to hurt her feelings, but I thought she must be joking. "I'm sorry. You surprised me. You actually believe there's a ghost?"

"When I was a little girl, none of us would go near the house. All my friends said it was haunted. Of course, it didn't help that Mrs. Thornly was an ornery old lady, scowling at us through the window whenever we dared to step on her lawn."

An old, empty house with so much history could easily spawn stories of spirits and specters. Add in small town rumors, and a death or two, and you had a haunted house. I thought of the marketing opportunities. 'Thrills and Chills at the Haunted Tearoom.'

"Irma never said anything about ghosts. Neither did Harold."

"Not everyone believes," she said. "And why would Harold bring it up if he didn't have to? He wouldn't risk chasing a potential buyer away."

I counted myself among the unbelievers, and I didn't want to end up in a long discussion about magical thinking. "Thanks for mentioning it, but I'm not worried." I stood. "I think I'll go for a walk while I'm waiting to hear from Harold and the mechanic."

"We're expecting rain later. You might want to bring an umbrella."

I managed to slip away when another guest came down the stairs and diverted Sarah's attention. The fog had turned into a thin mist, and I followed the sound of the ocean until I arrived at a picture-postcard sight.

The waves beat against boulders, sending spray ten feet or more into the air. A sunbeam broke through the fog and sparkled on the water. Far to the north, I spied a lighthouse I hadn't noticed, and beyond it, cliffs rose from the water.

I again found myself drawn to the pink and purple Victorian that I hoped would soon be my home, and I soon stood across the street admiring it. My phone rang. Harold explained the cat rescue had other offers they wished to review before accepting mine.

"Very well," I said calmly. I smelled something fishy, and it wasn't coming from the ocean. I decided to call his bluff. "I'll just call First Century Realty in Somerton and ask them to submit the offer for me."

After a long moment of silence during which I imagined Harold watching his commission shrink in half, he stammered, "There's no need to do that."

"I think perhaps there is. If you like, I'll wait an hour before making the call so you can see what you're able to accomplish in the meantime." I hung up before he could come up with any other excuses.

I climbed the wooden steps, examining the rose bushes covered in red, pink, and white buds ready to burst forth. Stepping onto the porch, I slipped into an old rocking chair to wait.

Forty-five minutes later, I received a call from Harold. "The board has decided to accept your offer. I'm preparing the offer paperwork needed to get the ball rolling. They've also agreed to rent you the home until close of escrow. I'll meet you at the house in an hour if that's suitable."

"That will be suitable. Thank you."

Harold arrived right on time. He unlocked the front door and stepped aside to allow me to enter. The interior seemed even more magical than when I'd seen it only the day before. I hadn't noticed the cornices over the windows or the carvings on the staircase rails or dozens of other intricate details I would no doubt discover over the coming weeks and months.

I hid my excitement as much as I could. He'd drawn up the papers to formalize my offer and open escrow, and I was assured the sale included all the contents, which were listed in an addendum.

Being more interested in the house than its contents, I briefly glanced at the pages-long list, which included various furniture items, lamps, and a variety of other items. I stopped when I reached the page detailing the kitchen contents.

"How old are the pots and pans and kitchenware?" It could save me quite a bit of money if they were still usable.

"Fifty, sixty years, I would guess," he said. "They were used for the restaurant for many years, so I'm not sure what condition they'll be in. We have an antique shop in town if you want some advice about how to get rid of whatever you don't want to keep."

"I'll keep that in mind."

Remembering the incident from the night before, I asked about Bob Shimp and his claims on the house. Harold assured me he'd looked at the so-called will.

"Whether his mother intended to leave the house to him or not is immaterial. The Thornly sisters were joint tenants in the home. That's how their father wanted it. Under a joint tenancy, the death of one owner automatically transfers the property to the survivors, or in this case, a single survivor —Barbara."

"I'm still surprised his aunt didn't leave him something."

"They had a falling out years ago," Harold said. "They never reconciled."

He reached into his pocket and pulled out a key ring with three keys. "One key for each front door and one for the rear. There may be other locks in the house, but these are the only keys the trust could locate." He handed them to me. "Enjoy your new home."

I CALLED to check on my car, and got a gruff response from a man who said he'd just gotten to work and what did I expect? For once, the slow pace of this town didn't bug me. After all, I had all the time in the world.

I returned to the B&B and called my bank for the wire transfer. Once the trust had the money, I hoped for a short escrow. I ordered groceries online to be delivered to the house the next day from Somerton, the nearest town with a full-sized grocery store. Along with staples like flour, sugar, and coffee, they had a surprisingly broad selection of premium loose teas, and I might have gotten a bit carried away. They even had Devonshire cream for the scones I planned to bake, so I ordered two jars. I justified the splurge by telling myself it was part of my research for my new tearoom.

Tuesday morning, I awoke at dawn, excited to start my new life. After checking out of the B&B, I said goodbye to Sarah and headed out. When I'd woken Sunday morning, I hadn't even heard of Serenity Cove, and now I was about to move into my new home. I took the scenic route by the water, rolling my suitcase behind me.

Lugging my belongings up the front steps, I unlocked the door and stepped inside. I took a deep breath to take in all the scents and smells of my new home and began coughing. The house had plenty of dust to go along with its history.

Something moved and I gasped. On the staircase landing sat a tiger or perhaps a leopard. It was a very small leopard, but not knowing much about wild animals, I thought it was best not to approach it. Laughing at myself, I realized it must be a stuffed animal, and I'd imagined the movement. Before I reproached myself for overreacting, it moved again. I dialed the real estate office.

Harold sighed. "It's just a cat."

"It doesn't look like a cat." I took a step closer, and it gave me an imperious glare. "And even if it is, it doesn't belong here. Come get it, please."

"You'll want a mouser," he said.

"A mouser?" I heard the pitch of my voice rise and took a deep breath. I didn't want him to think I was panicking. "The house has mice?"

"Not if you have a cat. Every house in town has at least one. It's the only way to control them."

"You don't understand," I explained. "I'm highly allergic to cats and dogs. My mother once had to rush me to the hospital because I had a near fatal reaction." She told me the story whenever I asked if we could get a pet. Thankfully, I had been too young to remember the ordeal.

After another ten minutes attempting unsuccessfully to convince him to take the cat away, I hung up and decided to take matters into my own hands. I found a box in the kitchen and carried it to the stairs.

As I climbed the first step, the cat's whiskers twitched. It turned and gracefully climbed the rest of the steps to the second floor, looking over its shoulder to check on me before heading down the hall to the back of the house. Whether he or she must have been making sure I stayed far behind or making sure I followed I couldn't tell.

At the end of the hall, the cat slipped through a door I hadn't noticed before. A closer look showed the door fit into the wall invisibly. "How interesting," I murmured.

Through the door, a narrow set of wooden stairs led to the next level. It should have occurred to me earlier that the house had an attic.

Near the top of the stairs, I peered into the dim attic. Dust motes swirled in thin beams of light from grimy windows. Tables, chairs, and lamps were stacked on top of each other haphazardly along with wooden crates and cardboard boxes.

I took the last few steps and placed one foot gingerly on the bare wood floor to test it. I'd briefly reviewed the list Harold had provided but didn't expect such lovely pieces. There were several elegant wingback chairs and a pair of leather club chairs along with two Tiffany-style table lamps. Most of the furniture appeared in good shape, though in need of a good cleaning and dusting.

Stacks of vintage-style dining chairs leaned up against the rear wall. I knew little about antiques, but that didn't matter. They must have been used for the restaurant and would be perfect in my tearoom.

The cat jumped onto a Windsor chair and curled up, very much at home.

"I'm so sorry I can't let you stay," I explained. Even if the cat couldn't understand my words, I hoped my meaning would come through in my voice. "You see, I have a severe allergy to cats." I remembered my mother using the word 'severe.' She even implied it could be life threatening. It seemed odd that my eyes weren't itchy, and I didn't feel the slightest hint of a sneeze coming on. Perhaps it was a different kind of allergy and I'd soon break out in hives.

This was my chance to catch the creature off guard and grab it, but I'd left the box one floor below. I doubted the cat would willingly let me pick it up and carry it back downstairs.

At the other end of the room, I spotted a china hutch. If I wasn't mistaken, it was an Irish dresser. The dresser was nearly four feet wide with open shelves on top and would be perfect for displaying merchandise. I imagined teapots and teacups sharing the shelves with canisters of exotic teas and beautiful linens.

For now, old books assumed every available space. I spotted copies of classics like *Tale of Two Cities* and *Pride and Prejudice*. A cookbook caught my eye and I pulled it out, blowing the dust off the top, which made me cough.

When I recovered, I read the front of the dust jacket. "*More Modern French Cooking,* by Chef Emile Toussaint." I turned it over to see a photo of a handsome, dark-haired man with a chef's hat. His smile was both friendly and condescending. I tucked it under my arm to take downstairs, thinking there might be a recipe or two I could use in my tearoom.

I'd ask Irma what to do about the cat later. Perhaps the rescue who was the recipient of the proceeds from the house would take the cat. I took the first step on the stairs back to the second floor when it made a noise.

"Mee. Yow."

Not "meow." I mean that's what it must have been, but it sounded like an impersonation of a cat. I gave the animal a long look and could have sworn it smiled at me. If it wasn't a baby tiger, it was one strange cat.

CHAPTER 5

*A*fter digging in my suitcase, I found a few bedraggled teabags and made a cup of Earl Grey tea. The sweet scent of bergamot reminded me of my mother who first taught me about different types of teas including this one, named after a former British Prime Minister. In the midst of a chaotic childhood with a free-spirited, unreliable mother, there were moments of calm and delight. Whenever I heard her in the kitchen humming, I knew she was having one of her rare, good days. She often emerged with a tray of tea and sweets for an impromptu tea party.

Pushing aside the bittersweet memory, I went through the kitchen cupboards, discovering copper pots and pans along with well broken-in cookie sheets and cake pans. A cast iron cookie mold reminded me of one my grandmother used to make corn muffins.

When I opened one of the lower cabinets, I let out a squeal. An entire set of cornflower blue, enameled, cast iron cookware hid in a corner cabinet. I turned it over expecting it to say Le Creuset, but instead, it said Descoware. Yet another thing to learn about.

A drawer next to the range held a rack full of sharp-looking knives. I opened more drawers, finding every kitchen tool and utensil I might want and quite a few I'd never seen before. After going through the entire kitchen, I made a note of the items I would need to buy--a few more cookie sheets, a food processor, and a microwave oven.

The doorbell rang, and I rushed to greet a friendly, young delivery person with my groceries. After putting the perishables in the refrigerator, I made myself a grilled cheese sandwich and ate it while I surveyed the various teas I'd bought. I finally settled on English Breakfast tea and brewed a pot. An old favorite, it would feel familiar and comforting with a dollop of milk.

I took my mug to the front parlor area and pulled a chair over to the bay window to take advantage of the view. The lawn, green and lush, stretched from the porch to the street. Across the street, the ocean crashed against the rocks, throwing spray high into the air. I blew on my tea, still too hot to drink, and opened the cookbook. Considering the title was *More Modern French Cooking*, I assumed it must have been the follow-up to a previous edition.

The author's name, Emile Toussaint, didn't ring any bells, but since it had been published in 1960, that didn't surprise me. The only chefs I knew who might have been alive back then were the famous French chef Escoffier and Julia Child.

I flipped pages, stopping at a random recipe. Vichyssoise. As a child, I wondered why anyone would want cold soup. Back then, French cooking was quite popular, especially among housewives. For all I knew, my mother might have bought one of Emile's cookbooks.

Goosebumps crept up my arms. Drafts and inefficient heating were the price I had to pay for living in an old house, but nothing a few warm layers wouldn't fix. After retrieving my sweater and a small throw blanket from my room upstairs, I returned to the cookbook, hoping to find something warm to cook for lunch, but the complicated instructions for even a bowl of soup gave me second thoughts. A grilled cheese sandwich sounded tasty, not to mention quick and easy.

Stepping back into the kitchen, I found an elegant, silver-haired man in a chef's hat leaning against the counter holding a glass of wine. Not only was it a bit early in the day to start drinking, but he appeared much too comfortable in my house.

"What are you doing here?" I demanded.

The chef gave me a smile that seemed familiar somehow. He took a slow sip of his wine as he faded away. I blinked hard several times. Great. Now I was seeing things.

Thankfully, I'd arranged for healthcare through a San Francisco medical group. I hadn't been to the doctor in two or three years, and it wouldn't hurt to get a checkup. They managed to fit me in the following Monday, less than a week away.

CHAPTER 6

The mechanic delivered my car after lunchtime with two new tires. I carried the boxes holding my belongings from the trunk into the house. The clothes and personal items went upstairs, leaving the three remaining boxes in the middle of the parlor. It wasn't much, but I'd decided to start a new life after all, so why lug around all my stuff from my old life?

One box held my teapot collection. After telling myself I was foolish and sentimental for bringing them with me, it seemed like fate I hadn't donated them with the rest of my castoffs. There weren't nearly enough for the tearoom, but I looked forward to searching for more, going from shop to shop and visiting local flea markets.

The furniture that came with the house was sufficient to furnish my upstairs living quarters, but I'd want and need a lot more pieces for the main floor. First, I'd need to take inventory of the items in the attic. No time like the present.

I climbed the two floors of stairs to the attic. If I kept going up and down the stairs, I might be able to skip the gym completely. Taking a look around, I pulled a heavy box full of odds and ends over to the wingback chair and sat down.

"Yowrrr."

The cat sat on the floor in front of me with an indignant expression on his face. I never knew cats could be so territorial.

"I'll only be a minute," I explained, inspecting a vintage wall clock. It wasn't ticking, but new batteries might fix that. I held it up. "What do you think? Not for the tearoom, but maybe for the kitchen?"

Not surprisingly, I didn't get a response. Impatient with my delay in relinquishing his chair, the cat jumped up on me. In my shock, I nearly dropped the clock. He crawled in circles on my lap as if trying to find a comfortable spot, finally squeezing in the small space between my thigh and the side of the chair. He closed his eyes, and I felt a vibration against my leg.

What were the first signs of an allergic reaction? From all the antihistamine commercials I'd seen, I remembered watery eyes, itchy throat, runny nose, but I didn't feel any of those symptoms. I made a mental note to ask the doctor what signs to watch out for.

Not sure what the cat would do, I reached out and gave it a little stroke, and the purring got louder. I leaned back in the chair thinking how lovely it felt with a cat by your side, warm and happy. Then, concerned I might skip all the warning signs and go directly to anaphylactic shock, I hurriedly grabbed the items I'd picked out to take downstairs. I turned back at the door to see the cat curled up in a ball with his little whiskers twitching in his sleep. Too bad I was allergic. I could get used to having a pet.

I'd hoped to bring that chair downstairs, but since he seemed to have claimed it, I returned to the attic and found a different chair and a coffee table. It took two more trips to carry them down to the main floor. The minor exertion had me breathing hard, and I reminded myself of my vow to get back into shape.

I arranged the furniture by the fireplace where a small stack of wood lay ready for my first fire. It had been a long time since I'd started one, but I had vague memories of my mother opening the flue and balling up paper under the logs. It took several tries, but I eventually had a nice fire crackling and hissing in a friendly, reassuring way, and the kettle on the stove.

While waiting for the water to boil, I unpacked my teapots, each one holding a special memory. Some were too special to use. My klutziness meant I couldn't be trusted with anything valuable and fragile, and in my mind, sentimental value trumped dollar value every time. I chose a plain white teapot with built-in infuser, the most practical choice.

With a cup of Darjeeling tea by my side, I opened my laptop and began researching. I had a lot of decisions to make. First, I pulled up pictures of tearooms around the world, and made notes of what I liked. By the time I'd emptied my teacup, I had two pages of notes I'd distilled into a shopping list.

I didn't find online shopping as much fun as browsing antique stores in person, but it was certainly efficient. I found a complete set of Princess Di commemorative plates, and before I knew it, I'd bought them. Before making any additional impulsive purchases, I thought it would be wise to put together a budget including furnishings and decorations.

A tapping on the door took me out of my reverie, and I stood up to let Irma in. Thankfully, her multicolored mermaid wig was gone, replaced by a fedora.

She glanced at the three boxes on the floor. "I hope I'm not interrupting your unpacking."

"I've always traveled light. I spent so little time at home, I figured there wasn't any point of accumulating stuff. I'm glad you stopped by. Do you know a good locksmith?"

She chuckled. "There's only one of anything in this town. That's if you're lucky." She pulled out her phone. "Call Mark."

"Thanks." I entered his number into my phone. "I'd also like the name of the cat rescue. There's a cat in this house."

"Whisk."

"Excuse me?"

"The cat's called Whisk."

"Who names a cat after a kitchen utensil?" I wondered. It sounded like something a chef might do, but I dismissed the thought.

"Rename him if you want," she said. "It's no skin off my nose."

"I might do that." I wondered if the cat knew his name. He might not want me to change it. "Would you like to join me for a cup of Darjeeling tea? It's one of my favorite black teas, grown in the Himalayan foothills. Tea has a fascinating history--did you know?"

"You don't have any coffee?"

I sighed. "How do you take it?"

I'd bought ground espresso beans hoping I could figure out how the cappuccino machine worked, but all the knobs and dials confused me. Opening one of the cupboard doors I spied the jar of instant coffee mocking me. It would have to do for now. I put the kettle on to boil and soon returned with a mug of coffee, along with cream and sugar. Irma picked up the cookbook, turning it over and staring at the author's picture on the back.

"Where did this come from?" she asked.

"The attic. Why? Have you heard of him?"

"Heard of him? I had a huge crush on him when I was seventeen. But that was before he disappeared."

According to Irma, in the late sixties, Norma, Bob's mother, turned the main floor of Thornly house into a French restaurant and hired Emile Toussaint as head chef. Handsome and worldly, he charmed all the local women, including Irma.

Irma took a sip of coffee, put it down, and leaned back in the chair as if getting ready to tell a long story. "Let me start from the beginning, or at least not from the middle."

"The two sisters lived in the house—Norma in the upper floor and Barbara downstairs. When Barbara got married, I was eleven, which would make it 1956, I think. My family wasn't invited, of course, although all the best families were. The Thornlys were practically royalty in this town."

"Is this a long story?" Her eyes narrowed, which I took as a warning. "Please, go on."

After a dramatic sigh, she continued. "As soon as Barbara moved out to live with her new husband, Norma tore down the walls on the main floor and opened Maison Rose, luring Chef Emile from a swank restaurant in Beverly Hills. People came from miles around to experience his gastronomical creations."

"I guess I'll have to try some of his recipes." My tearoom would serve sandwiches and scones, but a mini quiche or daily soup would be a nice addition to the menu. Plus, with so few restaurants nearby, I would be eating at home most nights. I might as well learn to cook gourmet dishes instead of living on grilled cheese sandwiches and frozen dinners.

Irma must have noticed my mind had wandered, because she cleared her throat to get my attention. "I was sixteen when I got a job here. They started me in the kitchen, but Chef said I was too beautiful to be stuck in the back. Of course, my head was turned by having a handsome, worldly man like Emile Toussaint calling me beautiful. I became a hostess, and Norma gave me some of her old dresses." Irma got a dreamy look in her eyes. "She had the most exquisite clothes from Paris. And magnificent jewelry. She'd been involved with a prince or archduke or something who gifted her with emeralds and diamonds and rubies. I sometimes wondered if people came for the food or to see Norma. She lit up the room."

A dark cloud passed over her eyes.

"What is it? Did something happen?" I asked.

"All good things must end. It was so long ago, I'm sure nearly everyone from those days is long gone." She gave me a wry grin. "I'm too darn stubborn to die."

From what little I knew about her, I didn't doubt it, but I wanted to know more about the chef and why he'd gone missing. "What happened to Emile?"

She stared out of the window, no doubt remembering those far away times. "He disappeared one day. Never came back."

"What do you mean, disappeared?"

She shrugged. "He was here one day and the next he was gone. The rumor was he'd run off with one of the women in town. She was married, so you can imagine what a scandal it was."

In a small town like Serenity Cove, it must have been all anyone talked about for months. "What happened after he left? Did the restaurant stay open?"

"Yes, Norma hired another chef. It was never quite the same. And then..." she winced.

I leaned forward, eager to hear the rest of the story. "And then, what?"

Irma stared into her coffee cup, but she seemed far away. "It's gone cold."

"Would you like another cup?" I asked, although I was impatient to hear the rest of the story. "Or I could heat it up for you."

"No, I need to get to the restaurant and get ready to open." She handed me her half-empty cup.

"Irma, what happened after Emile left?"

She stood. "Norma got married."

I had no doubt there was more to the story. "Did you still work at the restaurant?"

"No." She walked to the front door. "I left town to have my baby."

CHAPTER 7

I felt as if someone had stolen a book from me just as an important plot point was about to be revealed. Clutching my cup, I watched her walk to the sidewalk and turn down the street toward the Mermaid Cafe.

I called the number Irma had given me, and Mark said he'd be happy to stop by in half an hour to change all the locks. I'd taken the key hidden under the rock, but who knew how many copies were floating around. Small towns were like that, and I could imagine Barbara handing out keys like candy.

Refilling my mug with the last of the tea, which was now lukewarm, I made a note to buy tea cozies both for me and the tearoom to keep the teapots warm. I'd also like a new teacup for everyday use. Drinking tea in a thick mug didn't seem right.

I gulped the last of the cold tea and made a new pot. My mother had taught me so much about tea, but I had more to learn if I wanted to become an expert by the time my tearoom opened. I picked out a jade oolong tea, something I'd never had before. It was deep green with large, tightly rolled leaves. I read about the history of oolong teas while I waited for it to brew

Following the instructions, I scooped some of the bright green rolled leaves into one of my smaller pots. After heating fresh water to 165 degrees, I poured it over the leaves, then discarded the liquid. I filled the pot a second time and let it brew for less than a minute, then poured myself a cup. The taste, fresh and bright, had a touch of floral sweetness and the aroma hinted of lilies.

Curling up by the window with the cookbook, I sipped my tea and perused the pages. Each recipe sounded more delicious than the last, and with all the butter, cream, and other rich ingredients, I was glad there were no calorie counts listed. I had turned the page to the hors d'oeuvres when the doorbell chimed.

I opened the door to a handsome man with dark hair holding a clipboard. The sleeves of his chambray shirt were rolled up, revealing tanned, muscular arms. Was this my locksmith? The day had taken a turn for the better.

"I'm Mark Nazari." His deep voice exuded warmth. "We spoke on the phone?"

"Come in." I stepped aside, checking him out as he entered the room. Nothing wrong with looking, my mother always said.

"Would you like a cup of tea? I'm drinking jade oolong tea, but I have others to choose from. I wanted to try a gunpowder green tea from an estate west of Hangzhou, China next." My enthusiasm for sharing trivia took over, and I might have gotten carried away. "Chinese green teas tend to be milder than Japanese, and gunpowder is one of my favorites. It's called that because the leaves are rolled into little pellets."

"I'm more of a coffee drinker, ma'am, but thank you for the offer."

My sales skills must have atrophied with disuse. I supposed I'd want to figure out how to use the cappuccino machine ASAP or *tout de suite* as Chef Emile Toussaint might have said. After I explained I wanted all the locks changed, Mark wrote out an estimate. It seemed reasonable, so I asked him how soon he could do the work.

"Right now, if that's all right with you."

In half an hour, he'd changed the locks on both front doors and the back door. He also checked all the windows, which he said appeared to be secure as long as I remembered to keep them locked.

"Of course, someone could easily shatter a window if they wanted to gain entrance." He must have seen the concerned look on my face, because he smiled and added, "Not that that sort of thing happens in Serenity Cove."

I nodded, somewhat reassured. "Thanks for coming so quickly. I'll sleep much better now." Except for worrying about someone breaking in. "Maybe I should install a security system."

"Not a bad idea."

I had a thought. "Do you know a local handyman? I asked my agent, but the company he referred me to is in Somerton, and they're booked up for months. Besides, I'd rather work with someone local."

His eyes narrowed. "Harold gave you the referral?"

"Yes."

He shrugged. "I'm the local handyman. You might have some reservations since Harold didn't see fit to recommend me, but I can offer you plenty of references."

"That won't be necessary." I smiled. I didn't know what reservations Harold had when it came to Mark, but I doubted they had to do with his skills or professionalism.

"Thank you, ma'am."

The only people I knew who called women ma'am, were

southerners and ex-military. I didn't detect an accent. "What branch of the military were you in?"

"Army, ma'am. Served in Afghanistan."

"Thank you for your service," I said sincerely, knowing how much our troops often gave up serving our country. "How did you end up in Serenity Cove?"

"Married a woman from here," he said. "When we got a divorce, she came back with our son to be close to her folks. Didn't let me see much of him back then."

"But that changed?"

He nodded. "She got remarried and moved to Seattle. My son wanted to stay here and finish high school, so I moved here. The good thing about being a handyman is you can find work pretty much anywhere."

"I bet. Let me know when you can stop by again to go over everything that needs to be done. The major work will have to wait until escrow closes, but that shouldn't take long."

"I'll stop by tomorrow, if that's okay." When I nodded, he turned to leave.

"Wait." I had something I wanted him to check out right away. "The walk-in freezer won't open. Can you take a look?"

He followed me to the storeroom and pulled on the freezer handle as if a big strong handyman could open it when I couldn't. He took a closer look before concluding it was locked. "Have you checked all your keys?"

Harold had only given me keys for the exterior doors. "Can you make a key?" I didn't know if the freezer was in good working condition, but I'd like to know one way or another before opening day.

He shook his head. "It's so old, I don't have a blank that would fit it. I can put in a new lock if you'd like."

I agreed, and Mark went out to his truck, returning with the new lock. I left him to work drilling the old lock out, and twenty minutes later, he called for me to take a look.

The inside of the freezer had shelves with pull out drawers and adjustable trays. I could stock up on anything and everything I wanted. I never thought having my own walk-in freezer would be so exciting.

"Let me show you something." Mark indicated the inside door handle. "It's broken, so you'll want to keep the freezer locked until I can fix it. I'll order the part as soon as I get back to the shop."

"Okay."

"Don't go into the freezer until I get it fixed, understand? You could get trapped inside."

"Got it." I figured waiting a week or so wouldn't kill me. "But can we plug it in, so I know if it works or not?" I had no idea how long it would take to order another one, and somehow, after living my entire life without an enormous freezer, I couldn't imagine going without one any longer than I had to.

Mark squeezed behind the freezer and plugged it in. It began to whirr and hum, which sounded promising. He locked the door and handed me two keys on a small ring. I hung one on a hook on the wall next to a stack of cast iron skillets in various sizes and put the other in my newly designated junk drawer.

We returned to the front room, where we could see the sun dipping below the horizon through the front windows. The day couldn't be over so soon, could it? I glanced at my phone.

"It's seven o'clock," I said with surprise. "I'm sorry to keep you so late."

"No problem," he said, handing me a card. "Let me know if you have more work for me in the future."

"I hope you have a lot of openings in your schedule. I've got plenty to keep you busy."

Hungry, but too tired to make dinner, I threw the sheets from my new bed into the washer, ate a bowl of cereal, then curled up by the fire while they dried. I carried the warm linens upstairs, changed into pajamas, and climbed into bed.

As I closed my eyes, I thought about the handsome handyman and his soft, comforting voice. Before I knew it, I drifted off to sleep.

CHAPTER 8

I woke the next morning to a bright, sunlit room. As I rolled over, not wanting to leave the warm bed, the light dimmed as if the sun had ducked behind a cloud. After a moment, I remembered where I was, and felt my face break into a grin. My house. My tearoom. My new life. Looking out the window, I watched gray clouds float leisurely by. I hoped the clouds and drizzle were an early spring feature and the sun would come out to stay soon.

After a quick shower, I went through my clothes for something to wear. Irma had a point when she compared me to a librarian. In fact, few librarians I'd met had clothes as boring as mine. As the proprietor of a tearoom, I'd need a whole new wardrobe, but I had no idea where to start.

I soon made my way downstairs, made a cup of English breakfast tea, and took another look at the French cookbook. A recipe for Potage Parmentier caught my eye, even after I translated it and found out it was nothing more than leek and potato soup. It could have been called hot Vichyssoise, but at any rate, I was dying to try it for lunch. I made a shopping list including the ingredients for the soup along with other groceries I needed and drove to the only market in town.

Pulling into a space in the middle of the block, I found myself in front of Serenity Antiques. It couldn't hurt to take a quick look, so I ducked inside. I'd need more furniture for the tearoom, and if I could find vintage pieces at a good price, I'd prefer those to reproductions.

The shop was tiny, with tables, chairs, and lamps stacked on top of each other, and smelled of furniture oil. A narrow path led through the shop, and at the back a doorway led into the attached shop next door. I stepped inside a less crowded space nicely set up with displays of lamps, small furnishings, and accessories.

A mannequin wearing an antique dress caught my eye, and I had leaned closer to admire the detailed stitching on the bodice when the figure moved. I jerked back.

"I'm sorry," the mannequin said. She thankfully turned out to be a real person and not another figment of my active imagination.

"That's okay," I laughed nervously, recovering from my startle. "I didn't think you were real. Your dress is stunning."

She smiled proudly. "I collect vintage clothing. This dress is from the early nineteen hundreds. I would never wear it outside of the shop."

"I wouldn't think there would be many places you could wear it without getting weird looks."

She grinned. "I'm used to weird looks. I'm not going to let them stop me from dressing the way I like. Life is too short to wear boring clothes."

I looked at my own outfit which consisted of gray trousers and navy-blue sweater and then back to her. She didn't seem to notice or care that my style was the epitome of boring.

"I have plenty of reproductions to wear outside of work," she said. "This gown is far too fragile for the real world."

This young woman, barely more than a teenager, appeared as fragile as the gown she wore, but I told myself not to jump to conclusions.

"Is this your shop?" I asked.

She gave her head a small shake. "My father's, though he's given me this section to manage. He specializes in furniture and other large pieces, and I handle all the smaller items. Are you looking for something in particular?"

A glass counter ran along one side of the room, and I peered inside at the costume jewelry, watches, and cigarette cases, repurposed as business card holders. "Do you carry teacups?"

"Yes, we do," she said. "There are a few in the back by the books. I keep most of them put away because they get so dusty. And also broken." She laughed, a cheerful sound I found charming. So many young women were jaded and cynical, but she seemed as innocent as a child. I reminded myself again not to make assumptions.

"I'm opening a tearoom, so I'll need plenty of cups and saucers plus a few more teapots. I'm planning on interspersing new ones with vintage."

She seemed taken aback. "You're the woman who bought the old Thornly house?"

"You seem surprised."

"It's just, I don't know." She gave me another of her warm smiles. "You don't look like a high-powered executive."

I chuckled. The rumor mill worked fast in this town. "I'm not anymore. I'm a high-powered tearoom operator. My name's April."

"I'm Jennifer. Let me show you the teacups I have out."

She led me toward the rear of the shop, where the back wall was lined with shelves full of books. Some appeared quite old. "I don't suppose you have any cookbooks by Emile Toussaint. I understand he was a local chef."

A man wearing a sweater vest over a rumpled shirt appeared from the other room, glaring at her through thick glasses. "No, we don't have any of his books," he informed me, then turned to Jennifer. "Jennie, it's time to close."

"Dad, I'm helping a customer." The whine in her voice transformed her from a young woman to a teenager. She turned back to me. "We close from noon to one for lunch."

I gave her a smile, ignoring her father's rudeness. "I need to get going anyway. I'll come back another time and look at your teacups."

"Nice meeting you." Jennifer said.

I turned to her father, ready to introduce myself, but his scowl made me change my mind. I said goodbye and headed for the exit.

The grocery store stood two doors down. It appeared tiny from the outside, and I didn't expect much but had a pleasant surprise when I stepped inside. The white walls, gleaming stainless-steel shelves, and bright lights gave it a sparkling-clean atmosphere, and the narrow store seemed to go on forever. Their small produce section had all the basics, but no Belgian endive or English cucumbers. I bought a pint of juicy looking strawberries that I knew I'd find a use for.

I checked the aisles for clotted cream, not expecting to find it. Happily, I did find heavy cream that wasn't ultra-pasteurized. I'd heard it could be used to make homemade clotted cream, and I wanted to try it out. The nearest British grocery was two hours away in San Francisco, so if I could make my own it would save me time and money.

In one aisle, I found a passable selection of premium teas. I'd have to talk to the store manager to see about ordering a few more varieties. I'd prefer to support local businesses as much as possible.

In the back, I found the deli counter the innkeeper had told me about. Not sure how long my soup would take to prepare, I ordered a turkey and provolone sandwich on a French roll. The woman behind the counter told me the bread came from Molly's bakery.

Heading toward the checkout, I remembered Whisk. I didn't know much about cats, but I did know they needed to eat, so I picked up a bag of kibble, hoping he would approve of my selection.

Introducing myself to the cashier, I asked if the owner or store manager was on the premises.

"Oh, you're the new lady who's opening the tea shop," the woman said, sounding astonished at the idea.

"I am," I assured her. "I thought I should talk to them about the supplies I'll need to purchase when I open."

"Carol!" she called out loudly, and in a moment a woman with orange-red hair emerged from the back. "This lady wants to talk to you."

Carol gave me a worried look, as if prepared for an unhappy shopper. I guessed her to be older than I but younger than Irma. But then, almost everyone was younger than Irma.

After I explained why I'd asked to speak with her she brightened. "Welcome to our town," she said with a warm smile. "Make up a list and I'll see what I can do. We're limited by what our distributors can get us, but I'll do my best."

When I arrived home, I went straight to the kitchen impatient to start making the soup. Having never prepared leeks, I followed the directions carefully, washing the leeks thoroughly and trimming off the roots and the greener part. The remaining pieces were white and light green, and I sliced them thinly. My knife went through all the layers of the leeks in a satisfying way.

The butter melted slowly in the saucepan over low heat,

and I smashed the garlic and tossed it in. Since the soup would be pureed, there was no need to mince it, not one of my favorite tasks. Next, the leeks went in the pot and I stirred them and put the lid on. That gave me ten minutes to peel and thinly slice the potatoes which went into the pot along with some fresh sprigs of thyme, and a single bay leaf.

The recipe called for homemade stock, but I wanted soup today, not someday in the future. According to the Emile Toussaint's cookbook, homemade stock took hours to prepare. Besides, it couldn't make much of a difference. I opened a large container of chicken stock and added it to the pot.

I heard a sound--something like the way my mother would click her tongue. I turned around to see what or who had made the noise, half expecting to see my apparition scolding me. I chided myself for being so jumpy. Old houses made plenty of sounds, creaking and groaning all day and night. I'd better get used to it.

It was time to add the cream to the soup.

"Hmm..." I mumbled to myself. "Milk would be much healthier. I bet it would still taste good."

A voice behind me called out, "Sacre bleu." I slowly and carefully turned around. There stood Chef Emile Toussaint in the flesh. Well, not in the flesh, but there he was, and he did not look happy.

The hairs on the back of my neck stood on end. "You're not real."

He scowled at me, folded his arms over his chest, and slowly faded from view.

The vision shook me. I reached for the cookbook and turned it over, scrutinizing the chef's photo. How had my mind conjured such a realistic replica of Emile Toussaint? The chef in my kitchen had more silver in his hair, but otherwise, he appeared identical.

CHAPTER 9

J took my lunch to the front room and set it on the table by the window, enjoying the view while waiting for my soup to cool down enough to eat. A car parked in front of the house, and a young woman got out. It was Jennifer from the antique store.

She seemed startled when I opened the door before she'd had a chance to knock.

"Hello," she said. Her puffy jacket made her appear twice as big as when I'd seen her before, and she carried a gift bag. Had this young lady brought me a housewarming gift? "I hope you don't mind me stopping by."

"Come in." I stepped back and let her enter. "Let me take your jacket."

Jennifer had changed from her vintage dress and now wore a white blouse with a Peter Pan collar and red capris. She'd pulled her hair into a high ponytail and added a red headband. She might have stepped right out of a fifties' movie, and I had the urge to offer her a milkshake.

"I made Potage Parmentier. Would you like some?" When she hesitated, I clarified it was soup, adding, "I got carried away and made a huge pot, so you'll be doing me a big favor if you have some. I'll never finish it by myself."

Jennifer agreed, and soon we were happily seated by the front windows with our soup and fresh bread. She must have been enjoying it as much as I was since she didn't say a word until the bowl was empty.

"That was delicious," she said. "I wish I could cook like that."

"It just takes the right cookbook." After carrying our dishes into the kitchen, I scooped my special rose tea blend into the infuser and filled the teapot with hot water. I carried the pot to the table first, returning with two teacups and the cookbook.

"Oh, I love tea," she said. "Especially when it's served in a pretty teacup. It tastes so much better than when it's in a mug or especially a Styrofoam cup, don't you think?"

"I do," I said. "Styrofoam absorbs flavor molecules making the tea less tasty."

"Really?"

"Really. Plus, Styrofoam is yucky and bad for the planet."

I poured the tea, and she brought her cup to her mouth. Before she drank it, she said, "What is that heavenly aroma?" She inhaled the rising steam. "It smells like roses."

"It's a special blend of Keemun tea and fragrant red rose petals."

Jennifer took a sip and sighed. "Delicious." Putting her teacup down, she picked up the cookbook. Staring at the cover, her voice soft, she asked, "Did you know he used to live in this town?" She opened the book to the dedication on the first page. "He worked in this very building when it was a restaurant. Listen to this." She read from the dedication page. "For Norma, without whose inspiration and support this book could not have been possible. Someday, I will find a way to express my appreciation."

"I learned a little about him from Irma," I explained. "But he lived a long time ago. I'm surprised you've heard of him."

She picked up the gift bag from the floor where she'd placed it. "We haven't had many famous people in this town. I think he's the only one, in fact." She handed me the bag.

"That's thoughtful of you, but you didn't have to get me a present."

"Look inside."

I pulled out two books. Modern French Cooking and Advanced French Cooking both by Emile Toussaint. "How wonderful. I knew there must be at least one more cookbook. Are these your personal collection?"

"You could say that. I pulled them out of the trash."

Jennifer must have noticed my surprise. She explained her father hated hearing the name Emile Toussaint and must have thrown the books away, but she'd found them and kept them hidden.

"When the chef disappeared, his mother—my grandmother—did too. Everyone in town said they ran away together. My father was six years old at the time."

"How sad for him," I said. "She never came back for him?"

She shook her head. "He never heard from her again. He can't understand why his mother could leave her own child. Do you have children?"

I nearly choked on my last spoonful of soup. "No." I dabbed my mouth with a napkin. "I always wanted a child, but it didn't happen. I was married years ago, and I planned to give up my traveling when we were ready for kids, but before that happened, he'd found someone else. I guess it was my fault for being gone so much."

She scowled. "Don't say that. He sounds like a jerk."

"Then I got engaged again, but it was too late for kids. I'm going to be fifty soon." I'm sure to this young lady, I seemed ancient.

"You're engaged?"

"No, he broke it off." My love life seemed like a broken record. I didn't want to talk about my failed marriage or engagement anymore. "Did your father ever try to find his mother? Or the chef?"

"I don't know. I mean, I tried to find her, so he could have some closure, but the trail went cold. Actually, that's not exactly right. There was no trail. It's like they both disappeared into thin air."

What kind of man had Emile Toussaint been to convince a woman to leave her young child and run off with him?

THE FOLLOWING MONDAY, I left early for the drive to San Francisco and my doctor's appointment. After explaining my symptoms, the doctor suggested I see a psychiatrist. I assured him I was completely sane, and perhaps an MRI was in order.

Some doctors don't like it when I suggest a course of treatment, but this one didn't seem to mind and agreed to refer me to a neurologist.

"One more thing I'd like to ask you," I said. "My mother told me I had a severe allergy to cats. Can you outgrow that?"

He shook his head. "Not likely, but it is possible. Have you been having allergic symptoms?"

"No, that's the thing. I've been around a cat, and I haven't felt any of the symptoms I would have expected."

"We can do a skin test right now and you'll know within fifteen minutes."

He asked about medications I'd taken in the previous two weeks before sending in a nurse to perform the test on my forearm. The test didn't hurt, and she told me I'd see a reaction in ten to fifteen minutes if I had a cat dander allergy.

Fifteen minutes later, she announced that it didn't appear I had an allergy to cats or dogs.

"Are you sure?" I asked. There were two possible explanations. Either I'd outgrown my allergy, or my mother had lied. I didn't want to think about which possibility was more likely.

On my way to my car, I called the neurologist office who fit me in that afternoon. Since it didn't make sense to drive all the way back home, I treated myself to lunch at my favorite seafood restaurant and took a walk along the Embarcadero.

Returning to the same medical complex, the neurologist asked a few probing questions. With an MRI scheduled for the following week, I got back in my car for the drive back to Serenity Cove.

When I arrived home, I went straight to the attic. "Whisk?" I called out. "Where are you?" No reply. "I'm not allergic to you after all. Isn't that good news?"

After waiting for several minutes, I headed for the stairs when I heard a "Brrr" sound. I turned back to see him peeking out from a box. "What is it with you cats and boxes?" I said with a laugh.

He gave me a chirp, or at least that's what it sounded like.

"I've never had a pet before. You seem pretty low maintenance, but maybe that's just because you've been on your own for weeks. Do you miss your…?" Owner seemed like the wrong word. "Do you miss your person?"

It was lovely to be able to visit Whisk in the attic without worrying about an allergic reaction. Once he even sat on my lap and let me pet him for a few minutes. He quickly decided he'd had enough and ran away to one of his hiding places. It would take patience to fully earn his trust.

I saw the chef often in the next few days, and started to get used to his presence, even talking to him. He didn't seem interested in speaking to me outside of his one outburst, but sometimes he'd nod or shake his head.

"I bet tarragon would be a wonderful addition to this dish." I would look over and see his head shake in disagreement.

"It tastes a little bland. I wonder if I should add more salt." Head nod.

I would miss him when he was gone. Having a hallucination to talk to was even better than talking to yourself, if less socially acceptable. I could talk to Whisk, but I'd have to go to the attic to do so. I'd occasionally leave the attic door open, but he seemed happy where he was.

After a trip to the grocers for a whole chicken, onions, garlic, and a variety of vegetables, I prepared my first roast chicken. It was juicy and delicious, and I vowed never to eat chicken any other way. Except for southern fried chicken. Or coq au vin.

That weekend, I went through all three of Emile's cookbooks, looking for more soups to try. I found dozens of recipes for various consommés. I remembered visits to classic French restaurants where thin soups were offered as starters, but I preferred something heartier.

A recipe for cream of chicken soup brought back childhood memories. My mother wasn't much of a cook, but she could heat up a can of soup as well as anyone. I nearly changed my mind when I saw I would need to make a béchamel sauce first. I didn't even know what that was. I looked up to see the chef raising his eyebrows at me in censure.

"I'll make a béchamel sauce another time. I'm hungry."

He folded his arms over his chest and sighed dramatically. I nearly laughed at his antics but pursed my lips to suppress my smile.

I finally gave in. "Fine."

The recipe yielded four quarts of sauce, but the chef seemed to go along with my decision to make a smaller quantity. The first step was to make a roux by melting butter in a saucepan and adding flour. It soon began to brown and give off a toasty smell.

"Non, non, non," I heard his voice behind me.

I turned and stared at him. "Are you talking to me? Or is that all you say? 'Sacre bleu' and 'non, non, non'?"

"I only speak when I have something to say, unlike some people. And you are ruining the roux." His haughty voice had a trace of a French accent.

"Is that so? Well, I'm following your instructions from your cookbook." If it didn't come out right, he should take some of the blame.

"For a béchamel, one prepares a white roux, heating the flour only enough to eliminate the raw taste of the flour, but not enough to darken the mixture."

I cleaned out the pan and started over, melting the butter and adding the flour. After a few minutes, I added milk to the roux slowly, stirring it until it thickened.

"That will do," the chef said. "You have prepared a passable béchamel, I should think."

"Thank you for honoring my sauce with your faint praise," I said, but he didn't respond to my sarcasm.

Over the coming days, between visits to city hall attempting to get my permits approved, talking with Mark about what work I would need done as soon as escrow closed, and making lists of everything I would need to buy for my new business, I made lots and lots of soup.

I filled up the refrigerator with containers and served soup to anyone who stopped by. Irma and Jennifer were especially appreciative and visited regularly.

Monday morning, I bid Chef, as I now called him, goodbye for now, and headed off for the MRI. The following day, the neurologist called to make a follow-up appointment for Thursday. "It's our procedure to go over the results in person, even if they're normal, so don't be alarmed."

Little did she know that I didn't hope for normal results. I wanted her to find something in my brain causing my hallucinations. Something easily fixed by a pill or a zap of radiation.

The next two days, I followed up on the myriad permits, going online, making calls, and filling out forms. Perhaps red tape held the town together, and if the various civil servants cut through too much of it, Serenity Cove would fall apart. No one had any urgency regarding the opening of my tearoom except me, and nothing I said or did sped up the process.

Thursday morning, as I left for the neurologist, my goodbye to Chef was a little melancholy. Honestly, I would miss him.

I waited in the exam room, reminding myself not to seem too pleased at the MRI results.

"We did find something, but I don't want you to be alarmed," she said in a soothing voice.

"Yes?" The hopeful sound in my voice could be interpreted several ways.

After giving me a concerned look, she read from a report. "There is a 1.3 centimeter in diameter focus of central hyperintensity in T2-weighted images consistent with cavernous angioma involving the right frontal lobe."

I waited to hear the English version. "And that means?"

"A cavernous angioma is a collection of little arteries and small little veins. They're benign, they don't do anything, usually, and they don't cause problems, usually."

"I see." Usually didn't mean never, so I waited to hear more.

"We'll want to repeat the MRI in six months, but in the

meantime, I'm going to refer you to a neurosurgeon. It will take at least a week for the authorization to come through and then you can make an appointment."

I left her office with a bounce in my step, humming a happy tune. It was the best news possible. The cavernous angioma must be what caused me to see my apparition, it was benign, and it wouldn't get fixed for at least a week or two.

Which meant Chef and I could keep cooking together, at least for now.

GROWING impatient as the days passed without any word from Harold, I left him a message to ask if my escrow would close at the end of the month as expected. Nothing seemed to happen in a timely manner in this town. Harold stopped by to update me on the status.

"I wanted to tell you in person," he said with a smile. "Escrow closes on Friday. We'll need about a thousand signatures, and the house will be yours."

I felt a grin take over my face. "That's wonderful!" Now all I had to do was get all the permits and once necessary repairs had been completed, I could open my tearoom. Also, there was the redecorating. Lots, and lots of wallpaper to hang and lights to hang. It would be unrecognizable by the time I finished.

"How do you plan to celebrate?" he asked. "I could take you out to the Longhorn Steakhouse in Somerton. It's not exactly gourmet cuisine but the food is good, and it's a whole lot classier than the Mermaid Cafe."

The offer surprised me, as well as the dig at the Mermaid Cafe, but I had other plans. "Thank you for the invitation, but I'll be busy preparing for the open house I've been planning ever since I first moved in. You're invited, of course, along with anyone else who'd like to come. I've already ordered several cases of champagne."

Was it my imagination that he seemed disappointed? If he was interested in me as anything other than a client, I hadn't been aware of it.

"Great," he said. "I'm looking forward to it."

As soon as he left, I called Mark to see when he could stop by to give me an estimate of the work that needed to be done before I would be able to open. I'd already filed for a business license, food service permit, resale permit and half a dozen other permits and licenses. I hoped by the time Mark completed all the improvements, we'd be able to open.

But for now, I had a party to plan.

CHAPTER 10

Once I chose the day and time for the open house--Sunday at one p.m.--I printed out about a hundred flyers on colored paper. First, I drove over to the grocery store, leaving them a stack to hand out to their patrons. Glancing at Serenity Antiques, I decided against going in. Jennifer's father would probably throw them in the trash the moment I left.

On the way back, I stopped at the Mermaid Cafe, and slid an envelope with fifty or so flyers through the mail slot with a note for Irma, inviting her and anyone she thought would behave themselves.

I drove to the downtown area, which consisted of a bank, a few offices, and city hall. The latter consisted of a one-story building about a half-block wide. I'd never seen such a small government building.

Stepping inside the lobby, I headed for the information desk. The woman took my stack of flyers and suggested I pin one up on the bulletin board. I invited her to the open house, but she politely declined, saying she'd be at church most of the day.

"Another time, perhaps," I said, and thanked her again before I left.

Back home, I curled up by the fire--my new daily habit--and opened up one of Emile's cookbooks. I found appetizers in two places. Near the front, I found hors d'oeuvres, while appetizers and snacks appeared nearly at the end, right before Desserts and Sweets.

Before I got to the recipes, I read the chef's "General Remarks." I read aloud in a haughty voice the content seemed to require.

"I regard cold hors d'oeuvres as counter to the dictates of common sense, and they are certainly injurious to the flavor of the soup to follow."

I chuckled at the condescending tone so unlike anything a modern chef might write. Didn't anyone have parties back in the fifties and sixties?

One recipe for cheese puffs sounded promising, and canapés, which the chef described as "nothing more than pieces of toast, grilled, buttered, and garnished in some way," sounded easy enough. My cooking skills leaned toward scones and sandwiches, which was why I felt qualified to open a tearoom. Fancy French cooking wasn't my strong suit, but with Emile's help, my skills had improved.

"Tea sandwiches," I said out loud. Of course. It was an afternoon party, after all. Why not serve a few samples of afternoon tea fare? I decided against baking scones. If they wanted to sample my prizewinning scones, they'd have to come back when we'd opened.

All day Saturday and Sunday morning, I worked in the kitchen preparing the food, though it didn't feel like work at all. At one o'clock, trays of little sandwiches sat on the kitchen island covered in plastic wrap along with four cookie sheets full of cheese puffs ready to be baked. I carried two dozen champagne flutes into the front room and set them up on the credenza where I planned to place the appetizers.

Pulling the cheese puffs out of the oven, I transferred them to a rack to cool. As the clock ticked away the minutes, I ate at least a dozen before I forced myself to stop. People never arrived at parties on time, but when the kitchen clock struck two, I started to wonder if anyone was coming.

I poured myself a glass of champagne. "Just one," I told myself, feeling my mood deflate and hoping the bubbly would lift my spirits.

At two-thirty the front door opened, which meant the first guest had finally arrived. I hurried from the kitchen to greet them, and found Bob Shimp standing inside the door with his hands in the pockets of his windbreaker.

"What are you doing here?" I asked. The man had accused me of stealing his house from him. I didn't feel the need to be polite.

"I heard about the open house," he said, taking one hand out of his pocket to push his glasses further up his nose. He seemed awkward, uncomfortable, and completely harmless. "I hoped you wouldn't mind."

I thought about telling him yes, I did mind, and he had a lot of nerve showing up at my open house after accusing me of theft. But he was my only guest so far. He might be the only guest for the whole afternoon, and I had made a lot of food. I liked leftovers, but there was a limit as to how many cheese puffs I could eat by myself before I developed an aversion to them.

Did everyone in town hate me so much they'd turn down free food and drinks?

Bob shifted his weight from one foot to the other, waiting to hear what I had to say. I smiled indulgently. "Would you like a glass of champagne?"

I brought out one of the trays of tea sandwiches and a

plate of cheese puffs. We nibbled on them and sipped our champagne, making small talk. He owned and ran the town's pharmacy, and after we'd discussed the weather, that seemed to be the only subject he felt comfortable talking about.

As my mind wandered, I thought of his mother, Norma. The few details Irma had divulged piqued my curiosity.

When I had a chance to change the subject, I took it. "I heard your mother was a wonderful hostess, and people came from miles around to her restaurant."

He managed a small smile. "She was beautiful. Like a vision," he said reverently. "I can picture her walking down the stairs, the picture of elegance. She went to Paris annually for the spring fashion shows and came back with trunks full of dresses and gowns. Each night she wore a different one." He gazed at the staircase as if she stood on the landing about to make an entrance.

I followed his gaze, hoping I didn't see her as well, and breathed a sigh of relief at the sight of Whisk surveying us from the landing.

"Hello, Whisk," I called out. "This is Bob."

Whisk narrowed his eyes and stared at Bob before turning back to me and shaking his head. I wondered what the cat meant, but then I remembered animals don't communicate via gestures. Still, I nodded back to let him know I took his warning seriously.

"That cat creeps me out," Bob said.

"Is that so?" I asked, wondering why someone would have such a strong reaction to a cat. "I rather like him."

Bob filled me in on the fascinating world of pharmacy science while I silently prayed someone else would arrive soon. I excused myself to put another tray of cheese puffs into the oven. When I returned from the kitchen, I sighed in relief at the sight of Irma stepping through the front door.

"Irma, come in." I reached out to take her coat.

"I am in." Taking a few steps into the room, she stopped and turned to me. "Where is everybody?"

"Bob's here," I said cheerfully.

Bob had stuffed a tea sandwich in his mouth, so he grinned and mumbled something unintelligible.

She scowled. "I can see that."

Her attitude improved as soon as I handed her a glass of champagne.

"Bob was just telling me about his mother and all her beautiful designer gowns, weren't you, Bob?" I hoped to get him off the subject of pharmaceuticals. Otherwise, I might need a prescription for a tranquilizer before I strangled him.

Hoping Irma would forgive me for leaving her with Bob, I went to take the cheese puffs out of the oven. I'd returned to my two guests when the doorbell rang. Jennifer stood on the front porch wearing a beaded chiffon flapper dress complete with cloche hat.

"Come in." I grabbed her arm and pulled her inside. "You look adorable." Before I shut the door, I viewed Mark coming up the walk and pointed Jennifer in the direction of the buffet. "Help yourself to champagne and food. Wait. How old are you?"

She grinned. "I'm twenty-two. I've never tried champagne before."

"Well, go get a glass. It's the cheaper, California kind, but it's still wonderful."

My handyman appeared handsomely dapper in a black pullover sweater and slacks. He gave me a warm smile that threatened to turn my knees to jelly.

I stepped onto the porch to greet him. "I'm glad you could make it to my open house."

"Is that today?" He reached in his satchel and brought out an envelope. "I heard you closed escrow, so I thought I'd bring by the itemized estimate you wanted."

Judging by the way he was dressed, I didn't know if I bought his explanation. "As long as you're here, you might as well get a bite to eat."

The little group chatted and nibbled while I tried unsuccessfully to avoid checking the time. By three-fifteen, I concluded my open house would not be the bash I was hoping for. At that point, I forgot I wasn't supposed to have any fun and started to enjoy the company.

Jennifer was delightful, seemingly naive and innocent, but I got the feeling she could stand up for herself. I became even more convinced when she told us about her martial arts classes.

"My father enrolled me in karate classes when I was in kindergarten. He wanted me to be able to protect myself. I loved it and started taking more classes and competing too."

Mark smiled. "Jen won the state championship a few years ago. My son and I went to see it in Sacramento."

Jennifer's cheeks reddened. "I won my division. It wasn't a big deal."

I had a feeling it was a very big deal, and for some reason, I felt better knowing she could protect herself. If I ever needed a bodyguard, I knew who I'd call.

We were going through the champagne quickly enough, so I went back to the kitchen to get another bottle.

Chef looked up from his skillet. "When does your party start?"

"Very funny." I pulled a bottle of champagne out of the refrigerator, and then decided to grab one more for backup.

When I returned to the so-called party, a dark-haired, elegant woman in sunglasses stood by the front door. She swept her coat off her shoulders, revealing a chic off-white pantsuit. She gave me a dazzling smile as she approached.

"You must be April May." She reached out to shake my hand. "I'm Kyla Bradley with WSTV Channel 12 news."

"How nice of you to come." If I played my cards right, maybe I could get them to do a feature on my tearoom.

She surveyed the room then turned back to me. "Not much to report."

Her comment stung, but I forced a smile and invited her to join the small group. She froze in her tracks for a moment as if something or someone had spooked her. For a moment, I wondered if she saw the chef too, but then I remembered he was my personal hallucination. The group greeted her, and she eagerly accepted a glass of champagne, downing half of it in one gulp.

"Thirsty?" Irma asked, but before Kyla could answer, Jennifer proposed a toast.

"Here's to April and her tearoom."

Irma added, "May it last at least a year, because that's what I've got on the over-unders."

I stared at her, dumbfounded. "You're betting on my business?"

"Just ten dollars," she said. "And I don't know why you're looking at me. Harold put fifty on under."

"Under?" I wasn't a gambler, so Irma explained the fine art of betting, while I felt my eyes glaze over.

When she paused to take a breath, I slipped into the kitchen for more puffs, which were being gobbled quickly. After arranging them artfully on a serving tray, as if it mattered, I set them on the credenza.

Kyla popped one into her mouth. "These are delicious. I can't wait to come to your tearoom if this an example of your cooking."

"Don't get your hopes up," Irma said. "The only thing

she'll be serving is those little sandwiches. And undersized biscuits."

"Scones," I corrected.

"Whatever," she said.

Bob strolled around the house with his champagne, no doubt comparing the current house to what he remembered. I felt sorry for him, kept out of the house where he grew up, but it wasn't my fault his aunt had cut him out of her will.

"How about a game of truth or dare?" Irma suggested. "You go first, April."

Great. This party was going from bad to worse. I tried to think of an alternative, but the group seemed to have ganged up against me.

"Well?" she prompted. "Truth or Dare."

Knowing Irma as little as I did, who knew what she would come up with for a dare. She might tell me to run down the street topless. "Truth."

Irma's eyes narrowed. "Why did you come to this town where you know absolutely no one?"

"It was purely accidental. Fate, you might say. I had two flat tires, so I decided to explore the town for the day and spend the night. Then I saw the house, this house. It seemed as if it was meant to be."

"No, I want to know the real reason."

"Stop it, Irma," Jennifer said. "She answered your question."

I wanted to know what she was getting at, but that could wait for a private conversation. "Your turn, Irma," I said.

She crossed her arms over her chest. "Dare."

A screech from upstairs stopped all conversation.

CHAPTER 11

"*W*hisk!" I ran up the stairs and looked up and down the hall. I heard noises overhead and headed for the door to the attic, my heart beating furiously. As I reached the door, it flew open, and Bob nearly ran into me.

"What the bejeezus are you doing in my attic?"

"I wassh just—"

"Just snooping? Or looking to steal something? I want an answer."

"No, I jussh wanted to take a look around."

Obviously, Bob couldn't handle his champagne. I pointed toward the stairs and demanded he leave. When he hesitated, I gestured more emphatically and raised my voice for good measure. I didn't care who heard me. "Get out of my house. Now."

"Fine, fine." He lumbered toward the stairs, and I followed him to the landing. Harold had finally arrived, and just in time. He stood at the bottom of the stairs looking up at us.

"I caught him sneaking around upstairs. Again." I gave

Bob a little shove to encourage him to finish his walk down the stairs.

Bob approached Harold. "I jush took a look around. Is there a law againsht that?"

"Yes." I went to the front door and held it open. "It's called trespassing. Please go." I waited for him to get the hint. He finally walked out the door, and I shut it firmly behind him.

"Is he driving home?" Harold asked. "He probably shouldn't be driving."

"How the heck should I know?" I was still outraged that Bob had been snooping. "Bob is not my problem. I thought you were going to talk to him, Harold."

"I'll check on him." He looked at his watch. "I need to get going anyway—It's already four o'clock and I've got a house to show. Sorry I couldn't stay."

While Harold went after Bob, Irma pulled me aside.

"I have to go and open the cafe. But first, what was that all about?"

"I caught Bob in the attic. I think he was looking for something, but I've been through everything up there. There's nothing but old furniture and books."

Jennifer heard us talking. "Some old books can be worth a fortune. Did you notice if you had any first editions?"

I shook my head. The thought hadn't occurred to me. "I'll check later."

"What if he already got what he was looking for?" Irma asked.

I doubted Bob's jacket could have held a book without my noticing. "I don't think so, but if he did, there's not much I can do about it."

"We'll talk later." Irma said her goodbyes and left.

Jennifer and Kyla had found seats by the fire, so I popped another cheese puff in my mouth and joined them.

"Did Mark leave?" I asked.

Jennifer shrugged. "I can help you go through the books later to see if any of them are valuable if you want. I only work two nights a week at a restaurant in Somerton, so I've got a lot of free time."

"That would be wonderful," I said gratefully. "You know, I've got a lot to get done before we open. Would you be interested in another part-time job? Come to think of it, I'm going to need someone to help serve after I open, too."

She hesitated. "I'm just a hostess. I've never been a server."

"There's nothing to it, trust me. Think it over and let me know."

A huge grin took over her face. "I don't need to think it over. I'd love to work here!"

I let out a happy sigh. Jennifer was a delightful young woman, and she was perfect for my tearoom. "Come by in the next few days, and we'll go over the details."

"I'll come tomorrow," she said eagerly.

I went back to the sideboard to make a plate of sandwiches, hoping the two women would help eat some and keep me from having too many leftovers. I placed the food on the coffee table in front of them before stepping outside onto the porch to look around. Would Mark have left without saying goodbye?

A light mist drew me back into the cozy house. "Is the weather always so cloudy and drizzly, or only in the spring?"

"It's called May gray," Kyla said.

"And it's followed by June gloom," Jennifer said with a giggle.

"I hope that's followed by July." I thought for a moment. "July blue sky."

Jennifer grinned. "It is, actually. You might get sick of all the sunshine."

"And all the tourists," Kyla added.

I doubted I'd get tired of the sunshine or the tourists,

especially if they kept my tearoom busy. For now, I would enjoy the gray skies and misty weather knowing sunny skies would arrive soon.

As I stood by the sideboard, putting plastic wrap over the remaining sandwiches, the front door opened. Mark had returned.

"Sorry, I had to make a phone call. Took longer than I expected."

I heard a noise from the back of the house coming from the kitchen or the storeroom. I turned to check if a visitor had come through the rear door, but the door between the kitchen and storeroom was now closed. For a moment, I wondered if the chef had closed it, and then chuckled at myself. Whatever ghosts could supposedly do, I knew hallucinations couldn't move things.

"Did you hear something?" I asked the trio.

Mark had just stuffed a puff into his mouth, and he merely shrugged which I took as a no.

Before I could go check on the noise, a man burst through the front door. He looked familiar, but something about his demeanor made me think twice about offering him a glass of champagne.

"Dad," Jennifer said. "What are you doing here?"

"What am *I* doing here?" he barked. "I told you I want you to have nothing to do with this woman." After a quick glare in my direction, he turned back to his daughter. "You're coming home now."

Jennifer threw her shoulders back. "I'm not a child. I'm twenty-two years old. You can't order me around."

"As long as you live in my home, you follow my rules." He grabbed her arm and led her out the front door. She shot a forlorn look at me before the door slammed behind her.

"Poor girl. Why does her father treat her like that?" I turned to see that Mark was my only remaining guest.

71

He held up a cheese puff. "These are delicious."

It wasn't even five o'clock. Shortest party ever.

"Are you busy tomorrow?" Mark asked. "I can stop by to fix the freezer door handle if you want."

"The only thing I have planned is figuring out how to untangle the remaining permits, licenses, and certifications from all the red tape. Stop by anytime."

I consolidated the remaining appetizers on one tray, carrying the rest to the kitchen. I squeezed the remaining unbaked cheese puffs into the refrigerator, wishing I could use the walk-in freezer.

When I returned to the front room, Kyla had returned, and she and Mark sat next to each other by the fire deep in conversation, perhaps even flirting with each other. And why not? They were two attractive single people, after all. Still, I would have liked a chance to get to know Mark better before he was taken off the market. Maybe if I hadn't forgotten how to flirt, I might have a shot.

The doorbell rang. A late arrival? The only thing worse than a party where everyone came late was one where people showed up after the party had ended.

I opened the door to a middle-aged, rotund man in uniform folding a black umbrella. I had an idle thought wondering where he'd found a belt that could go all the way around his massive belly.

"Hello, may I help you, Officer?" I hoped this was a friendly visit.

"Sergeant Carl Rawley," he said in way of introduction. He sniffed the air like a bloodhound. "I understand you are having an event."

I gave him a friendly smile. "Just having a few people over." You could hardly call my pathetic open house an event. I stepped aside to allow him to enter but held up a hand when I saw his muddy boots. "Wipe your feet, please."

His mustache twitched in apparent irritation, but he complied.

"May I offer you some appetizers?" I asked as he entered.

A moment of indecision flashed across his face. "You need a permit to operate a restaurant. Do you have one?"

I frowned. "You need a *lot* of permits, but I'm sure you already know that." The small-town bureaucracy frustrated the heck out of me. "I have my food service license, certificate of occupancy, and building health permit. I don't have my seller's permit or resale permit yet, but I'm not selling anything today."

He took a few steps toward the sideboard when he noticed Mark and Kyla sitting by the fire. They'd stopped talking but avoided looking at the sergeant whose gaze rested on their champagne flutes.

His eyes brightened. "What about a liquor license?"

Thank goodness Kyla spoke up. "I brought the champagne," she lied. "I hope there's not a law against bringing liquor to a party."

The sergeant scowled, and his gaze returned to the food.

I picked up the appetizer tray and held it toward him. "Help yourself, Sergeant."

He took a cheese puff and popped it into his mouth. Happy to see the officer enjoying my food, I hoped it would help put me on his good side. That hope was short-lived.

"I appreciate your hospitality, Ms. May," he said, shoving one more puff into his mouth and heading for the door. "But we don't take infractions lightly in Serenity Cove. Make sure you have all the permits in order before you plan any more events."

"I will, I assure you." I closed the door after him and turned to see Mark and Kyla watching me.

"That man," Kyla said, shaking her head. "Do you know he

once had my car towed because I was six inches into the red? Six inches!"

"Thanks for helping me out." Who knows what would have happened if he'd realized I had supplied the champagne? "How many police officers does this city have?" I wondered how many other officers would be watching me to make sure I didn't break any laws.

"None, actually," Kyla said. "The city council disbanded the police department back in 1996. We contract with the Sheriff's office, and Rawley is assigned to our city. He's the acting Sergeant."

"I see. I suppose there isn't a lot of crime in such a small town."

"The last census counted 963 residents," Mark said. "It doubles during tourist season."

Kyla chuckled. "He's not wrong. And that's not counting the crowds who come for the day. The county assigns a second officer for four months or so, and the city hires a temporary traffic enforcement attendant. They write enough parking tickets to pay for their salary along with whatever the mayor's latest pet project is. After last summer, she redecorated her office."

I couldn't wait for summer and an influx of tourists. "You two can stay and chat as long as you want, and please eat more appetizers. I'm going to start cleaning up."

I assured Mark and Kyla they didn't need to help me carry the trays, but they insisted. After the parlor had been returned to its pre-party appearance, I sent Mark off with a box of leftovers while Kyla stayed behind.

"I'd like to do a story on the opening of your tearoom," she said. "Would you mind if I stopped by tomorrow to discuss it?"

"Sure. There may be more people coming by tomorrow than there were at my party."

She gave me a wry smile. "Don't take it personally. It takes the locals a while to warm up to new people."

"I'm shocked, considering how welcome the locals have made me feel." No doubt she could hear the sarcasm in my voice. "I don't mean you, of course," I added as an afterthought, hoping I hadn't offended her.

"I know what you mean. I've been here twelve years, and I'm still considered an outsider."

"What brought you here?"

"Shortly after I graduated from college, I got a job writing for the Serenity Cove Sentinel, our local newspaper. I can't even tell you how excited I was. You'd think I'd been hired by the New York Times."

"From what I've heard, newspaper jobs aren't easy to get, even at small town papers."

She nodded. "It's even harder now. I thought I was starting a great career and I would transition to being a TV news anchor. A few years later, I got a job as a reporter for the local TV station, but all they let me do is fluff pieces."

"Like the opening of a tearoom?" Before she could answer, I assured her I wasn't offended that she considered covering my opening 'fluff.'

"One of these days, I'll get to do hard news, but I might have to change jobs first. I wish something more compelling would happen in our town, so I could get the scoop, but that's never going to happen."

"I like that nothing much ever happens in Serenity Cove," I told her. "Hopefully, that will make my opening a big event."

After Kyla left, I took a plate of tea sandwiches upstairs along with one of Emile Toussaint's cookbooks. The upstairs parlor faced the ocean, and I had a spectacular view of the whitecaps glowing in the light of the full moon. In spite of the chilly night, I opened the window a crack, so I could hear the crashing waves.

Nibbling on sandwiches, I flipped through the pages until I spotted a recipe for crepes. It triggered a memory of my mother on one of her better days making crepes and topping them with powdered sugar.

What else did I have to do with myself while waiting for permits and for furniture to arrive? Tomorrow morning, I would learn how to make crepes.

CHAPTER 12

I put the crepe pan on a low flame, pleased the kitchen had the right pan for every need. I poured the batter into the pan and swirled it until I had a thin pancake. Chef leaned against the counter, giving me a disapproving gaze.

"What? Am I making them wrong?" I asked. "I followed the recipe to the letter."

"The ingredients, perhaps. The technique, no."

I smiled, ignoring the possible insult. "Explain, then. What's wrong with my technique."

"First of all, one must allow the batter to rest. You did not."

I gave him a guilty look. "Mark's coming by any minute. I didn't think it would matter that much."

"Once you are fully trained and have mastered all of my methods, then you may begin to, shall we say, improvise. But never, ever change your technique merely for expediency's sake. That, my dear, is a recipe for disaster."

I thought that was an overly dramatic statement, but a

good pun. "You said first of all I should allow the batter to rest. What else did I do wrong?"

He coached me through pouring the batter into the hot pan, lifting it off the flame, and swirling it until I had a paper-thin crepe, and only then setting it back on the burner. I reached for the spatula to flip it over, but he held out his hand to stop me.

"Shake the pan from side to side to ensure it slides freely, then—" He mimicked flipping the crepe up in the air and catching it in the pan.

I watched him dubiously as he mimed the action again. Holding my breath, I made sure the crepe was slipping in the pan then flipped it up in the air. I exhaled as it landed in the pan safely. "I did it!"

After allowing the bottom to cook briefly, I slid it onto the rack next to the first. I had to admit it appeared more crepe-like than the previous attempt.

Five minutes later, I slipped the last crepe onto the rack as the doorbell rang. I hurried to the door where Mark held two takeout cups, presenting one to me with a flourish.

"I know you're a tea drinker, but I thought I'd take a chance and bring you a cappuccino."

I smiled at the thoughtful gesture. "It's a nice change from tea. I haven't gotten around to figuring out how the cappuccino machine works, but soon I'll be able to offer you a cappuccino when you stop by." Which I hoped would be often. "I made some crepes. Would you like to try them?"

"I just ate breakfast, but thanks."

"They're more like dessert crepes, or what the French call crêpes sucrées. I'm going to cut up some fresh strawberries to serve with them. Some people think you can only have dessert after lunch or dinner, but I don't approve of such narrow-minded thinking."

Mark laughed and agreed to try my crepe, so I directed

him to the table by the front window before returning to the kitchen to finish my preparations.

"You're acting the fool, throwing yourself at him that way." Chef stared out the kitchen window, clearly sulking.

"By serving him crepes?" The fact I'd hallucinated a jealous chef would be hilarious if I didn't have crepes getting cold and a guest waiting for me in the other room. "He's coming to fix the freezer handle. If I feed him, maybe he'll give me a break on the repairs." My to-do list already stretched about a mile long.

Ignoring the scolding apparition in the kitchen, I plated the crepes adding sliced strawberries and a dollop of freshly whipped cream and carried them to the table where Mark waited.

"Wow," Mark said appreciatively. "This looks amazing."

"Please," I said. "Dig in."

Once Mark had cleaned his plate, he leaned back in the chair. "Have you thought about opening for breakfast? The only places we have for breakfast are the hotel dining room and the bakery."

"Molly's bakery, right?" I needed to check that place out.

MARK OFFERED to help with the dishes but knowing Chef would be lurking and possibly making snide comments would take all the fun out of having a live man in the kitchen with me. I thanked him for the offer but insisted I could handle a few dishes on my own as he carried his plate to the kitchen.

"I'll fix the freezer handle then while you're cleaning up," Mark said. "If you keep cooking the way you have been, the refrigerator will be overflowing in no time."

"I think it already is." Besides the leftover appetizers from the night before, it held several cartons of homemade soup.

Mark disappeared into the storeroom, returning a moment later. "Where's the key?"

"On the hook. Remember? You saw me put it there."

I joined him and saw what he meant. The hook was empty. "Well, that's odd. I'll get you the spare."

Opening the junk drawer, I took out two notepads, some pens, and several granola bars, and finally found the second key, which I handed to Mark.

While the sink filled with sudsy water, I avoided looking at Emile. Was it weird that I liked the idea of my handsome imaginary friend being jealous of me? It had been a long time since two men had fought over me, even in my daydreams.

"April." Mark's voice was urgent. "You'd better come here."

"What is it?" I stepped through the door, wondering if the power to the freezer had been turned off and I'd be greeted with spoiled food, but it had been empty when we'd locked it. Moldy cheese would have been much better than what I saw.

A body lay face down covered in ice crystals, his face a pale blue. It would be hard to recognize anyone's features covered in frost, but I recognized the jacket.

It was Bob.

CHAPTER 13

*B*ob couldn't be the only person with a similar jacket, so I took a step closer to the body to double check. Shaggy hair, wire-rimmed glasses. Yep, it was Bob all right. I pulled my phone out of my pocket.

"Who are you calling?" Mark asked.

I looked at him like he was an idiot. "I'm ordering a pizza. What did you think?"

He took the phone from my hand and disconnected.

"Hey!"

He pulled out his own phone. "Dispatch is a hundred miles away. It's quicker if we call the police station directly."

He stopped talking when a woman's voice came on the other end of the phone.

"Pauline, It's Mark Nazari. There's been a—"

She interrupted him and he rolled his eyes.

"Pauline! There's a dead guy at Thornly House." Pauline said something I couldn't hear. "Yes, dead. No, I don't know who it is."

I waved my arms to get his attention. "It's Bob."

"Bob?" he repeated. "Bob Shimp? Are you sure?" He spoke

back into the phone. "April says it's Bob Shimp." Pause. "April May. The woman who bought the Thornly House." Another pause. "Yes, she's turning it into a tea place." He gave me a long-suffering look. "Would you send Sergeant Rawley over?"

He disconnected the phone and leaned back against the counter. "What an awful way to go. Freezing to death."

"I've heard it's quite peaceful as you enter hypothermia." Afraid I sounded too cheerful about the situation, I added, "But, of course, there's no good way to die. How the heck did he get into the freezer."

"Good question."

"And where did the key go that was hanging on the hook? Do you think someone unlocked the freezer and Bob went in for some reason? And he couldn't get out?" I had so many questions, but Mark didn't have the answers. "The door was locked this morning, right?" Of course, it was. Otherwise, why would he have asked me for the key?

He didn't answer right away. "I think so. I mean, I assumed it was locked, so I didn't try to open it. But I think… when I turned the key…" He frowned in concentration, then shook his head. "I'm not completely sure."

"After he left the party, Bob must have come around the back," I guessed. "Maybe he wanted to hide." I doubted anyone would be stupid enough to hide in a freezer.

I glanced at Mark's footprints on the dirty floor. After days of drizzle, the mud refused to stay outside where it belonged. Inspecting the floor between the freezer and the back door, I discovered a wide swath as if someone had drug something through a thin layer of dirt.

"What are you looking for?" Mark asked.

"Footprints. It might tell us whether he was alone yesterday when he went into the freezer. Someone could have closed the door behind him."

Mark grimaced. "To play a joke?"

"What kind of a joke is locking someone in a freezer?" I doubt that Bob thought it was funny before he froze to death.

"But only you and I knew the handle was broken and couldn't be opened from inside, right?"

"But if the door was locked…" I wished Mark had tried the handle before using the key. "I'll explain everything to the police, I'm sure they'll figure out who wanted Bob dead."

A voice behind me scoffed. "Not likely."

I swung around. Chef stirred a nonexistent pot with an imaginary spoon. In spite of knowing it was all in my head, I wanted to ask what he was making. I smelled garlic and my stomach rumbled even though I'd had breakfast. You would think seeing a dead body would blunt my appetite, but it didn't seem real.

"What's wrong?" Mark asked.

"Wrong? Oh, nothing. I thought I heard something. I'm a little jumpy."

"That's perfectly understandable." He reached out and gave my shoulder a reassuring squeeze. "You've had a shock. Would you like me to make you a cup of tea?"

"I need a whole pot," I said, my shoulder tingling where he touched it. "I'll make it. But what about you? You've had a shock too."

"I'll be fine." Mark went back into the storeroom while I busied myself with the tea kettle, ignoring Chef's running commentary.

"What do you know about this man? I don't like you being alone with him."

"Tough," I whispered. I was about to ask if he'd seen anything the previous afternoon or evening, before reminding myself imaginary friends make terrible witnesses.

83

"Do you know anything about his past? He could be a criminal, you know. Have you considered that?"

"Shut up."

Mark reappeared in the doorway. "What?"

"You probably should stay away from the freezer until the police get here. It might be best to stay away from the storeroom. In case his death wasn't merely an unfortunate accident." My gut told me it wasn't an accident. It was murder.

"I hadn't thought of that." He shifted his weight from foot to foot. "Do you think someone locked him in on purpose?"

A recent memory popped into my head. "Do you remember me asking you yesterday about the noise I heard? Do you remember what time that was?"

He shook his head. "Sorry."

I searched my memory. "It was after Bob and Harold had left. And Irma, I think."

"Around the time Jennifer's dad showed up?" he asked.

"Yes!" I thought back to the distraction Mr. Skilling had made, insisting Jennifer leave with him. "That might have been the murderer putting Bob's body in the freezer. If we can remember what time that was, it might help the M.E. pinpoint time of death. When a body is in a freezer, it's sometimes harder to tell when death occurred."

Mark frowned. "How do you know that?"

I laughed, momentarily forgetting about the dead body. "Everything I know about murder investigations I learned from T.V."

The doorbell rang, and I hurried to let the police in. Except it wasn't the police.

Irma appeared less pulled together than usual, wearing sweats and a red skull cap. Still, her shoes matched her hat, so I had to give her props.

"It's not a good time," I said.

She gave me a knowing look. "Because of the dead body?"

"How do you know about that? We only called the police five minutes ago. Do you have a scanner?"

She scoffed. "No, of course not. Nothing ever happens in this town. It would be a complete waste of money."

"Then, how?" The only ones who knew were Mark, me and the police. A thought struck me. "Pauline?"

"Don't go getting her in trouble." She pushed past me. "I heard you found Bob in the walk-in freezer."

I chased after her as she hurried to the kitchen. "Stay out. It's a crime scene."

She stopped at the kitchen doorway to look back at me. "A crime scene? He was murdered?" She spotted Mark. "Hello there."

Mark nodded a greeting. "Good morning, Irma."

She narrowed her eyes, pulling me aside. "How long has he been here? Since yesterday?"

I closed my eyes and told myself to breathe. "Mark came over this morning to fix the handle on the freezer. He found the body."

The doorbell rang again. This time it had better be the police. I opened the door expecting to see a team of law enforcement and crime scene personnel, but instead, it was Sergeant Rawley.

"I understand there's been a death in your house, is that correct?

"A murder," I corrected. I stepped aside so he could enter and looked past him toward the street. His patrol car was the only vehicle parked there. "Is the M.E. on the way?"

He scoffed. "I'll decide if and when I'll be calling in the coroner."

I stared at him dumbfounded. Did the sergeant plan on solving a murder single-handedly?

"Now, if you don't mind, I'd like to see the body."

~

Sergeant Rawley kicked Irma, Mark, and me out of the kitchen, so I carried my teapot and teacups along into the front room. I always found a nice strong cup of Darjeeling as eye opening as a cup of coffee, so I hoped it might win them over. Mark and Irma took the cups without argument, and I got comfortable in my chair, or at least as comfortable as one can be with a dead body in the other room.

I asked them where the rest of the police force was, which got a laugh from Irma.

"He *is* the police force. We've tried to increase the budget for another officer, but the city council always turns us down. I don't think Sergeant Five wants anyone else on his turf, anyway. He pretends he needs the help but never gives the council a good argument as to why they should hire someone.

"Sergeant Five?" I asked. "I thought his name was Rawley."

"We call him Sergeant Five by Five," Irma said. "He's as wide as he is tall."

"Insulting, but accurate. Is he a good investigator?"

Irma waved a hand dismissively. "The man's only good at giving out parking tickets and getting in the way. He's tried to close the Mermaid Cafe down plenty of times. Luckily, the locals come to my defense."

Mark interjected, "How would we know if he was a good investigator? There isn't normally anything to investigate."

"There were those burglaries a while back." Irma snickered. "He solved those, and it only took him a few weeks."

"I heard about that," Mark said. "It's not really a burglary when you leave things on your front porch or in your back yard."

"But he solved that case?" I asked hopefully.

Irma and Mark seemed to share a secret joke.

"What?" I didn't like being left out of the loop.

Irma grinned. "Turned out, it was a raccoon."

I collapsed back into my chair. "He's never going to catch this murderer, is he?"

"Never is a long time." Irma stood. "I've got to get going but let me know what happens."

The sergeant emerged from the kitchen. "I'll need to question you first, Ms. May. Do you have an area where I can set up shop for a few days while I'm completing the investigation?"

I cocked my head, trying to make sense of what he said. "You won't be working out of the police station?"

"Boiler's on the blink," he explained. "Cold as blazes in there. You can't open your business until we finish our investigation, so it makes sense to work here, if that's not a problem?"

He said it like it was a request, but I knew better than to say no. "Of course, you're welcome to work here, Sergeant. Make yourself at home."

I didn't mean it literally, but that's how he took it.

CHAPTER 14

Sergeant Rawley made himself comfortable in front of the fire. He'd asked Mark to wait, so he could question him, but he was taking his sweet time getting around to it. My stomach growled as lunchtime came and went.

After heating up a big pot of Potage Parmentier soup, I offered Mark lunch. Not wanting to be rude, I asked the sergeant if he'd like a bowl.

He slurped his soup eagerly. "I hope you'll be serving this soup in your restaurant. It's mighty fine."

"I'm opening a tearoom. I am considering offering soup with afternoon tea."

He frowned. "What about lunch or supper?"

"I have signed a non-compete clause with Irma, so I won't be able to serve dinner." It was a load of rubbish, but I was tiring of people asking me why I didn't open a restaurant.

"Well, it will be nice to have a new lunch spot." He picked up his bowl, tilting it to get the last spoonful. Only when he'd finished eating did he begin his questioning.

He pulled a small notebook from his pocket. "I hope you have a good lawyer, Ms. May."

My heart started beating faster. "What are you talking about? If you think I'm the murderer, you're on the wrong track."

"I was talking about negligence. This was no murder. You left the freezer door unlocked, knowing that it had a faulty handle and that someone could get trapped inside. I suppose you're lucky he has no relations, or they'd take you for everything you've got."

"It was locked. The latch was broken, so Mark locked the door and I put the key on a hook in the back of the room. Anyone could have unlocked the freezer and shoved Bob in."

His eyebrows came together in a snarl. "Are you implying that Mr. Nazari unlocked the door, allowing Bob to get stuck inside?"

"No." I fought to keep the irritation out of my voice. "I'm *implying* that Bob was *murdered*. Didn't you see the drag marks from the back door?" I waited for a response, but he flipped through his notes ignoring me. "Did you even look for footprints out back?"

"No need," he said. "This is an open and shut case of accidental death caused by a blatant disregard for safety."

I put my head in my hands. Which was worse? The fact I might lose my home and never get a chance to open my tearoom or a murderer walking around with no risk of being caught?

"I'll speak with Mr. Nazari now and then I'll head back to the station to file my report." He looked longingly at the fire, and I half expected him to agree with my murder theory just so he could stay by the fire eating my soup for a few more days.

I stood. "At least tell me there's a medical examiner coming."

He shot me a glare. "The coroner will be here shortly."

"Good." Maybe he had a few more brain cells than Sergeant Rawley

～

Since Sergeant Rawley couldn't be bothered to do a real investigation, I tip-toed into the back room to take another look at the floor. Great. The streaks I'd noticed before that had made me think Bob had been dragged into the freezer were obscured by Sergeant Rawley's footprints.

If Bob had been attacked in my storeroom, there would have been a lot of noise. Was Bob rendered unconscious, then locked in the freezer to die? Or had he been killed outside and dragged inside?

I didn't care for Bob, mostly because he kept snooping around in my attic, but that didn't mean I was happy about what had happened to him. Now that he was dead, I might never find out what he was searching for. I pulled out my phone and took pictures of what was left of the dirty streaks. Someone needed to look for footprints outside the back door, and since Rawley showed no inclination to do so, it would have to be me.

Quietly and unobtrusively, I passed them on my way to the front door. Rawley stopped speaking when he noticed me.

"Be right back," I said, breezily, before he could ask me where I was going.

The day had warmed, and leaves danced in the wind as I headed for the back yard. Muddy prints from the previous day would have dried and turned to dust by now. I wondered if important evidence was being blown away.

A sidewalk led from the driveway to the back door. Avoiding it, I stepped on the grass, so I wouldn't disturb any footprints. I couldn't discern any in the dusty cement, but I took close up pictures of the sidewalk, along with the concrete steps and door jamb. They might show something when I enlarged them.

Before today, I'd been too busy working on the inside of the house to take a good look at the back yard. I'd never even stepped inside the small, wooden garage. Who'd left the door ajar? Probably the gardeners I'd heard the other day. Thankfully, the trust had agreed to pay for upkeep until the close of escrow.

I stepped inside the nearly empty structure. In the dim light filtering through a single grimy window, I could make out a rack of tools—hoes, rakes, and trowels. As I turned to leave, a shape on the floor caught my eye. I stepped toward the shovel to put it back where it belonged but stopped before touching it. Was this a clue?

CHAPTER 15

I brought cookies and water for Mark and the sergeant. I took my time, putting the plate down and placing the glasses in front of them, hoping to pick up snippets of their conversation.

Rawley reached for a cookie before the plate even touched the table, popping it whole into his mouth. I handed him a napkin and waited for him to finish chewing. If I'd hoped my hospitality would allow me to learn anything, I was out of luck.

The sergeant cleared his throat and spoke to Mark. "You're free to go for now. I'll let you know if I have any other questions. You're not planning any trips out of town, are you?"

"No, sir." Mark stood and turned to me. "Thanks for the crepes and the soup, April."

I followed him to the door, and we stepped onto the porch. For a few moments, we stood side by side staring out at the ocean, as if in a moment of solidarity. I guess discovering a body together can do that to two people.

"Don't worry." His eyes were kind and reassuring. "I told

Rawley how you locked up the freezer and put the key on the hook behind the pots and pans. No one will believe this was your fault."

I gave him a wry smile. "I'm not sure anyone else has to believe it if Sergeant Rawley does." Perhaps he'd have to convince the district attorney, but I had no idea how that worked. I'd never been accused of a crime. I'd hadn't even gotten a parking ticket in years.

He took my hand, giving it a gentle squeeze. "Let me know when you want to get back to work on the house."

"Will do." Something began to reawaken, as if a memory of something I'd never had, but I did my best to stifle it. I didn't have time for a man in my life, at least not right now. An occasional friendly touch would have to do.

Besides, he might be a murderer.

MARK WALKED toward his truck as gray clouds darkened the sky, our few minutes of sunshine over for now. A white van emerged from the mist and headed toward us. As it pulled into the driveway, I mentally went through everything I had on order trying to think what might be arriving. A young Black woman jumped out of the van and headed my way wearing a white polo shirt and slacks.

Then I remembered the chairs. They'd been delayed for weeks, and every time I'd checked, they gave me a new delivery date. I hoped this meant they'd arrived early.

Mark gave her a wave. That was just like a small town where the handyman and a delivery driver would know each other. I wondered if there was anyone in town Mark didn't know.

"Hello, Mark," she called out as she headed my way, her

short, corkscrew curls bouncing as she walked. "How's the bursitis?"

"Much better, thanks," he answered before getting in his truck.

"Are you delivering the chairs?" When she gave me a funny look, I figured I'd guessed wrong.

"I'll be arranging a pickup, not a drop off." She smiled and held out her hand. "I'm Dr. Fredeline Severs."

I shook her hand. "You're the coroner?" I hoped I didn't sound too surprised. I chastised myself for assuming the coroner would be a man. From this close, Dr. Severs didn't appear as young as I'd first thought, but she couldn't be more than her early thirties.

"And the local M.D. The only one in town."

"Yes, I understand there's a rule there can only be one of anything in this town," I joked. "You're lucky the opening for doctor wasn't already taken."

"It was, but my dad let me work with him until he retired a few years ago, and then I took over his practice when he passed away."

"I'm sorry—" I began.

"It's been a few years, and he'd been sick for a while, but thanks."

"I'm April May. I bought this house, and I'll be opening a tearoom as soon as escrow closes, and I get all the permits straightened out."

"Not to mention getting the dead body out of your freezer." She paused, then asked. "Would you mind directing me to the body?"

I'd almost forgotten about poor Bob. "Of course, right through here."

She stepped into the front room, and the moment she and Rawley eyed each other, a frostiness filled the air.

"Sergeant," she said.

"Doc, thanks for coming. Bob Shimp's death is a clear case of negligence. Don't let Ms. May convince you otherwise." He scooted forward in his chair preparing to lift his substantial girth.

She held up a hand. "No need to get up, Sergeant. I think Ms. May can show me the way."

"I'm ruling it an accidental death," he called out before stuffing another cookie into his mouth.

The moment he turned away I made a face at him. Dr. Severs must have seen me because she chuckled.

I led her to the kitchen. "It was no accident."

She looked back at me then pointed toward the storeroom. "The freezer is through here?"

"Yes." I followed her, pointing to the marks on the floor. "I think his body might have been dragged in from outside. The only question I have is whether he was conscious when he went in the freezer."

The doctor glanced at me curiously, then turned her attention to the floor. "Interesting. What did Sergeant Five— Sergeant Rawley have to say about that?"

"He wasn't interested in anything I had to say. He thinks Bob accidentally locked himself in." I pointed at the door. "The handle is broken, so I've kept it locked. Mark came here to fix it today and found the body."

She crouched down next to the body. "It sure looks like Bob."

"That's what I thought."

"I'll take it from here," she said, which I took as a dismissal.

"If you need me, I'll be in the kitchen."

∾

WITH THE CORONER in my storeroom and the sergeant in the parlor, the kitchen seemed the logical place to pass the time. Waiting never came easily to me, so I decided to bake. I flipped through Emile's cookbook for something to have with my tea. But I knew what I really wanted.

Chef Emile appeared interested in my preparations. "It appears you are planning to bake. A tarte Tatin, perhaps?"

"I'm making scones."

"Scones?" he scoffed, his chin lifting ever so slightly. "Peasant food." He gave an exaggerated shiver.

"You can leave if you like. I've made scones plenty of times, and I can get on quite well without you."

"Go? Go where?"

I stared at him. "Go wherever you go when you're not here."

"But I'm always here."

I'D PUT the scones into the oven when I heard the coroner's voice. "Ms. May?"

I went into the doorway and peered into the storeroom where she stood next to the open freezer door. "You can call me April."

"Okay, but only if you call me Freddie. Or Doc. Either one is fine." She turned back to the body. "Ascertaining time of death is going to be a challenge. Before I fill in the sergeant, can I ask you a couple of questions?"

"Shoot."

"I understand you recognized him when you found him this morning."

"I recognized his jacket first. It is Bob, though, isn't it? Bob Shimp?"

"It sure is." She glanced at the body and gave a little shake of her head. "I'm surprised Mark didn't recognize him, but maybe he didn't want to take a closer look. Dead bodies tend to make some people uncomfortable. I understand he was at your open house last night."

I nodded. "I'd invited the whole town, but I didn't expect him to come. He showed up at two-thirty."

"In the middle of a big party, you remember what time he arrived?"

I chuckled. "It wasn't much of a party, to be honest. I started to think no one was coming when Bob finally showed up. This town doesn't exactly roll out the welcome wagon when new people move into town."

She raised her eyebrows, but I found it hard to think my words were a revelation.

"I must have looked at the clock every two minutes until Bob got here. I was relieved at least one person came."

"Even if he had accused you of stealing his house?"

I wondered if the sergeant had filled her in over the phone, or if this was another example of the efficiency of the local rumor mill. "You know about that?"

"Any idea what time he left?"

"Right about four. I found him sneaking around in my attic and kicked him out. Harold arrived and went after him to make sure he wasn't driving. We'd been drinking champagne, but he's the only one who seemed to have overindulged."

Freddie nodded, then passed through the kitchen, either to speak to the sergeant or go back to her van.

I stopped her. There was something I needed to know. "Did he freeze to death?"

"It appears so," she said. "But first someone hit him on the head."

"With a shovel?" I blurted out.

She shot me a suspicious look.

"There's a shovel lying in the floor of the garage," I explained. "The rest of the tools are lined up neatly. It seemed odd, that's all."

"Why were you checking the garage?" Before I could answer, she said, "Never mind. Show me."

Rawley looked up as Freddie followed me through the front room, but he said nothing as we passed by. I led her along the driveway to the back yard the way I had gone before.

"The side door was open. It was the first time I'd been in the garage, so the shovel could have been lying there all along."

She stopped at her van to grab supplies. Unlike the sergeant, Freddie wanted to preserve evidence. Maybe now that we knew Bob had been hit on the head, he'd take the case more seriously.

Freddie carried the shovel to her van before taking a closer look at the back yard.

She sighed. "There might have been evidence this morning, but now that it's been drizzling steadily for the past hour, I doubt I'll find anything."

"I have pictures."

Freddie turned to me and grinned. "I'm starting to like you, April."

CHAPTER 16

$\mathcal{I}$ got back to the kitchen as the timer went off. After taking the scones out and transferring them to a rack, I stood near the door while Freddie filled the sergeant in on her findings, hoping to catch part of their conversation.

The chef's voice interrupted my eavesdropping. "Will this be a regular occurrence? I never allowed anyone but staff to enter my kitchen. There seems to be no end to the people traipsing in and out this morning. Does the young woman have experience?"

"Yes," I said, confused by the question. "She's a doctor."

He sighed. "I meant to ask if she has culinary experience. Your lack of proficiency is likely to be a hindrance as we prepare to reopen the restaurant, and it would be helpful to have an employee with relevant skills."

"I'm opening a tearoom, not a full-service restaurant. And she's not a new employee. She's the coroner. Were you not aware of the dead body in the freezer?"

"Zut alors!" he exclaimed. "That is unacceptable."

"I had nothing to do with it, I assure you, and I don't expect it to happen again." At least, I hoped not. "Did you hear anything yesterday afternoon around four? Like noises in the back room?"

"There are far too many noises in this house since your arrival. I'd meant to speak with you about it."

"Okay, but what about yesterday?" I prompted. "Maybe you heard someone open the freezer door. Do you remember?"

He stared off into the distance, but was he thinking about my question or the best way to prepare a souffle? He stepped to the stove and began stirring an invisible pot. I was about to give up on him when he spoke.

"One does not put sacks of supplies in the freezer," he said. "One divides the contents into smaller quantities. Of course, I rely on the freezer only when necessary. Fresh ingredients are far superior."

"You heard someone?" I guessed. "Dragging something like a sack?"

The chef scowled. "Grunting and cursing under his breath. So uncivilized. But what do you expect from a deliveryman?"

"You're sure it was a man?"

"Do you think I cannot tell a man from a woman?"

It wasn't much of a clue, but knowing it was a man who dragged the body to the freezer was a start. I headed for the front room to let Freddie and Rawley know what I'd learned when I stopped and chastised myself. No way could I tell them how I'd come across the new information without both of them thinking I was crazy.

Retrieving the Devonshire cream and jam from the refrigerator, I ladled them into ramekins. Raised voices emanated from the living room—not shouting, but Freddie and Sergeant Rawley were trying to get their respective points across by speaking louder than the other. That never worked, but it might make it easier for me to eavesdrop.

Returning to my post by the door, I held up a finger to shush Chef.

Freddie said in frustration, "You can't possibly think she created all this evidence in order to divert suspicion away from her."

"That's exactly what I think," the sergeant barked. "I'm going to prove she murdered Bob."

I sucked in my breath. Was he talking about me?

"You didn't even think it was murder," Freddie protested.

Great. Now that Rawley finally agreed Bob had been murdered, he'd landed on me as his number one suspect.

"There was no reason to think it was anything other than a tragic accident at the time." He sounded defensive, as well he should.

"Which you were ready to blame on April without any evidence."

"It was a clear-cut case of negligence. Now that we know someone locked him in there on purpose, she's the only possible suspect. Several people witnessed an altercation between her and the victim."

"Fine. You proceed with your investigation, and I'll come to my own conclusion. And I have no doubt my findings will show someone other than April murdered Bob."

I carried the tray of scones, clotted cream, and jam to the parlor and laid it on the coffee table where Freddie and Rawley sat by the fireplace. Handing the sergeant a napkin, I held back telling him what an idiot he was. No reason to give him more reason to want to lock me up.

"This looks lovely, April," Freddie said, giving me a smile. "I don't think I've ever had scones before. They are scones, right?"

I nodded. "With Devonshire cream and raspberry jam, the

way the English like it. It's up to you how you layer it. Jam topped with cream is Cornish-style, but I like it with the cream first then jam, or Devon-style. You can break off bits of scones and add the fixings as you go or make a little sandwich."

She prepared a chunk of scone Devon-style and took a bite. "Oh, my. That's delicious." She addressed the sergeant. "Isn't it delicious, Sergeant Rawley?"

He'd just stuffed half a scone in his mouth, so he gave her a grunt which seemed to imply he agreed.

Freddie finished her scone and her discussion with Rawley, and then collected Bob. I nearly asked if I could help, but the idea of touching a dead body gave me the heebie jeebies. She lowered the stretcher, slowly pulling him onto it before raising it and rolling him to her van.

As FREDDIE DROVE AWAY, another van pulled up to the curb with a WSTV logo on the side. "Oh, no." I'd completely forgotten about Kyla Bradley stopping by to talk about a feature story. I'd let her know this wasn't a good time.

"April," Kyla called out as she climbed out of the van holding two cups.

A man with a camera emerged from the other side of the van. I held up one hand to stop her, as if you could slow down a force of nature like Kyla with a gesture. "You can come in, but no cameras."

"Sure, no problem." She walked over to the cameraman and after a short conversation he returned to the van.

I held open the door for her and stepped aside to allow her to enter.

She handed me one of the cups. "I hope you like mocha cappuccinos. Molly's makes the best."

"Thanks." One of these days I'd have to stop by the bakery and check it out.

Rawley had taken another big bite of scone, judging by his inflated cheeks and crumb-covered uniform.

"Sergeant Rawley, I'm glad you're here." Kyla stepped forward and the sergeant rubbed his hands on his pants before shaking hers. "I got you coffee from Molly's just the way you like it." She handed him a to-go cup. "I'd like to get a statement from you."

He removed the lid and took several gulps of coffee before answering. "I have no statement at this time."

"I understand. How about a little information off the record?"

"Off-off the record?" he stammered. "The last time I spoke to you off the record I nearly got fired."

Kyla gave me a look as if to say, "Look what a small-town reporter has to put up with." I sympathized, but I also didn't blame Rawley for clamming up. I had no doubt she'd take advantage of any scoop she could get, whether it was off the record or not.

"I guess I'll have to talk to Dr. Severs then. I wanted to give you credit for any advances in the case, but if you don't want to brief me…"

His face reddened as he decided what to do. "Fine," he said. "Sit down."

I hovered nearby, pretending I was busy cleaning non-existent crumbs off the sideboard, hoping to hear what the sergeant had to say to Kyla. I thought I was being subtle, but he noticed and glowered at me.

"May we have some privacy?"

"This is my house, you know." I put my hands on my hips, but I knew if I didn't leave, they'd find somewhere else to talk.

After briefly considering going upstairs and watching TV,

I remembered the cable still hadn't been hooked up. I went back into the kitchen, where Chef appeared to slice leeks, though they were just as much an apparition as he was. The rhythmic way his knife sliced through the layers mesmerized me. He ignored me, and for a moment I wondered if he knew I was there. I couldn't see him all the time. Did it work the other way around?

I chuckled, reminding myself he was a hallucination. Then he spoke.

"Many, many aspiring chef de partie would seize the opportunity to observe and learn at my side. You behave as though I were a fry cook at a, how do you say? A greasy spoon! Do you wish to improve your skills or not?"

I smiled. I might as well humor him and see what my subconscious had to offer in the way of cooking techniques.

"Sure, Chef. What are we making?" I flipped through the cookbook to see what looked good.

He stopped chopping and scooped the leeks into an imaginary bowl. "It is imperative for every chef to perfect, as much as feasible, the preparation of stock."

"Stock? But I bought several boxes of perfectly good chicken stock."

Turning toward me, he lifted his chin haughtily. "Stock *est le plus important*. If it is bad, or merely mediocre, it is hopeless to expect a satisfactory result."

His passion about something so mundane surprised me. Was I channeling my desire for passion through him? I'd always been envious of those who pursued their goals with intensity and devotion. I couldn't remember feeling that way about anything, at least not since I was a girl.

"No theories or recipes," he continued, "not even mine, can take the place of experience."

He talked to me as if I was his assistant or perhaps the

chief bottle washer. Still, even though I had a lot to get done before opening day, I also had plenty of free time.

I could think of better things to make than stock. Something I could serve in my tearoom. Sausage rolls. Eclairs. I had a long list of potential recipes, and I couldn't wait to try them all.

When I returned to check on Sergeant Rawley, Kyla had left. I explained I needed to go out, but the sergeant didn't budge. I wondered how long I'd be stuck with him in my house.

"Lock up if you leave, please." I gathered my shopping list and keys and headed out.

I drove to Somerton to visit their full-size grocery store, knowing the little market in town wouldn't carry everything I needed. Strolling down each aisle, I came across their wonderful selection of teas. I spent half an hour picking out several to buy. Besides the tea, I came home with sausages, puff pastry, and more baking supplies.

"Anybody home?" I called out as I entered, thankful no one answered. I hoped the sergeant wouldn't return, though I doubted I'd be so lucky. For all I knew, he'd be back the next day to arrest me for murder.

I carried my groceries into the kitchen, but I didn't see the chef. "I don't need him nagging me," I muttered, although the kitchen felt empty without him. I opened his cookbook, flipping through the pages, but all of his recipes confused me with their old-fashioned terms and limited instructions. It was as if they were written for people who already knew how to cook. Not that I was a complete novice, but I had no idea what the difference was between braising and roasting.

Putting his book down, I retrieved the recipe for sausage rolls I'd found earlier. According to the recipe, between prep time and cooking time, they wouldn't be ready for at least an hour. I glanced at the clock.

Or I could go to the Mermaid Café and eat dinner at a civilized time. I grabbed my purse and jacket and locked up.

CHAPTER 17

*W*hen I stepped inside the Mermaid Café, all noise and movement seemed to stop as I made my way to what I now considered my regular table.

Irma strolled over and pulled up a chair. "The soup du jour is lentil soup with ham."

"No soup." I tilted my head toward the bar where several of her customers pretended they weren't watching me. "I guess everyone's heard about Bob."

"I haven't told them a thing, but of course everyone in town knows. You look like you could use a nice steak. Medium rare?"

"Sounds good. And a beer, please. Whatever you have on tap is fine." It had been a long day to say the least.

Irma stood, but paused next to my chair before putting in my order. Lowering her voice, she said, "Sergeant Five warned Pauline not to say anything, but it was too late by then. She told everyone you left the freezer door unlocked and it's your fault Bob's dead."

"Well, she's not up on the latest gossip." I considered the

wisdom of confiding in her, but the whole town would know by morning. "Bob was murdered, and Rawley thinks I'm the one who did it. It's bad enough no one's ever going to come to my tearoom, but now I have to deal with being accused of murder."

"Wait and see. Nobody liked Bob." She turned and headed for the kitchen.

Mark entered and after nodding in my direction, joined some friends at a booth. I guess it was okay to do work for an accused murderer, but socializing went too far.

Irma returned with a beer and a small glass of amber liquid. "Whiskey. I figured you could use it after the day you've had."

"Thanks."

"Why thank me? I'm putting it on your bill."

I smiled, wondering why Irma put on such an act pretending she wasn't a nice person. Not that nice would be the first word I'd use to describe her, but she did care, even about me, someone she'd met weeks ago.

I drank the whiskey in one shot, feeling the liquid warm me from the inside out. The steak, served with asparagus and mashed potatoes, hit the spot. The craziness of the day began to fade into the background. Everything would work out. It always did.

Either that or I'd be going to jail for the rest of my life.

A THICK DRIZZLE coated my hair and jacket by the time I got home, and I headed straight for the fire and its dying embers. As soon as I added a log or two, I'd have a lovely warming blaze.

A noise from the stairs made my heart race for a moment

before I saw what had made the sound. Whisk. Darn. I'd forgotten to feed him.

"Whisk. I'm so sorry."

The cat blinked and turned to go up the stairs. I hurried into the kitchen, poured some kibble in a bowl, and followed him up to the attic. Picking up the bowl I'd left there that morning, I placed the new bowl on the floor, but he backed away from me. He didn't look afraid, but perhaps he wasn't comfortable around me yet.

"Waiting for me to leave before you eat your dinner?" I asked. "I'm not going to try to catch you, I promise."

"Brrraaah," he trilled, twitching his tail.

"How am I supposed to interpret that?" He wanted something from me, but I had no idea what it might be.

I turned to go back downstairs when Whisk cried out, more insistently this time, "Yowrr." He turned and ran to the far end of the attic.

"What is it, Boy?" I followed him, hoping he didn't want to show me the corpse of some creature he'd caught. I had hoped having a mouser, as Harold had said, would mean I'd never have to see a critter in my home.

Had someone moved the furniture? I tried to remember how I'd left it but dismissed the idea. I noticed a beautiful desk for the first time, the type with lots of drawers and cubbies. Taking a closer look, I admired the finish and the detail. I lifted a corner to see if I'd be able to pick it up. It was heavy! I'd ask Mark to carry it downstairs for me.

A scratching sound made me turn toward the wall. The cat pawed at a board that had been pulled or pried off. I'd have to ask Mark if he'd been looking for termites, but I didn't see any of the telltale signs of wood shavings. Not that I was an expert on such things.

Or had someone else pried the boards off the wall? In

addition, several drawers had been pulled wide open. Had Bob been searching for something when I caught him in the house my first night in town? Is that why he was in my attic the day he died?

"Who was up here, Whisk?" I asked, but he simply purred in response and rubbed against my leg.

"If they come back, you have my permission to scratch their eyes out."

I GOT out of bed on Tuesday morning, dressed, and shuffled downstairs, feeling at loose ends. Now that my walk-in freezer was a crime scene, I could add that to the many reasons for my delayed opening. I'd applied for all sixteen permits the town, county, and state required, and they were painfully slow to get approved. I had a feeling this town ran on red tape, with charges adding up each time a form needed a correction or refiling.

But there was one thing I could accomplish today. I could learn to operate the cappuccino machine. I approached it tentatively, eyeing the knobs and dials.

After several minutes, I gave up trying to figure it out on my own and turned to the internet. None of the videos or instructions matched the vintage machine. Telling myself I'd rather have a cup of tea anyway, I put the kettle on, and opened the cabinet. A cellophane-wrapped package of white pearl tea caught my eye. I'd forgotten buying it at the grocery store the day I first met Jennifer.

The package called it "the most delicate of all white tea." The buds, hand rolled into pearls were supposed to unfurl while steeping. I placed a few into my one-cup infuser. When the water boiled, I turned off the burner and waited a minute for the water to cool. White tea, unlike most black teas, was best brewed between 170 and 185 degrees Fahrenheit.

After the tea had steeped for five minutes, I set the infuser aside for a second steeping. I inhaled the steam and took my first taste. The delicate flavor had a sweetness I didn't expect, and I knew I'd discovered a new favorite tea.

Starting work on my ever-growing to-do list, I left Jennifer a message to ask when she would be available to start work. She'd be a big help with the decorating along with other more mundane tasks. With her experience at the antique shop, I hoped she would take over the merchandise displays.

She arrived later in the morning in a circle skirt and saddle shoes, her hair in a high ponytail. She carried a large cardboard box.

"Good morning," she said, her ponytail bouncing. "I hope you don't mind me stopping by without calling first. I brought you some teacups to take a look at."

"Wonderful." I took the box from her and set it on a table. "I could have come to the shop."

"Yeah, well, my dad…" her voice trailed off.

Reaching into the box, I unwrapped the teacups one by one, setting each one on its matching saucer. Many were traditional, with roses or other flowers, but a few had fun, modern designs. I turned one over.

"Most of them are made in China," she said, almost apologetically.

"I don't want to serve tea to customers in the good cups. If one of these breaks, I'll be disappointed, but it won't be the end of the world." I pulled the last cup from the box and counted twenty all together. "These are lovely. How much for the whole box?"

Grinning, Jennifer said, "I knew you would like them." She suggested a fair price, and I quickly agreed.

"That's a good start on the cups. Now all I need is teapots, plates, silverware, and tables."

"And some chairs for the people to sit on?"

"We've got lots of chairs in the attic, but we'll probably need more." I showed her my notebook and the to-do list I'd started. "Lucky for me, Mark is available to help with the redecorating—painting, wallpapering, and putting up shelves, things like that. And he's working with a contractor to make one of the entrances wheelchair accessible."

"And the restroom?"

"Yes. I got a list of everything required by the regulations, but I'm not going to rely solely on that. I want everyone to feel comfortable coming here for afternoon tea. The menus will have large print for anyone with vision issues, which I know anyone over forty will appreciate." I picked up a few teacups to carry into the kitchen to wash.

Jennifer followed my lead, and we soon had all the cups on the kitchen counter. I filled the sink and began washing the china cups.

"What about vegan or gluten free options?" she asked.

I sighed. "That's going to be a challenge. I can make vegan scones with coconut milk, and there are plenty of vegan options for sandwiches, but I'll have to get creative to come up with gluten free recipes. I know for some people, what they choose to eat is a matter of preference, but for others it's a necessity.

Jennifer picked up a dishtowel to dry the teacups and saucers. "I have a friend with a nut allergy and going out to eat is always so stressful for her."

"I want my tearoom to be calming." I gave her a smile. "I'm hoping you'll help taste test all my recipes."

She grinned. "I think I'm going to like this job."

"Speaking of jobs, when are you available to start?" My

excitement was getting the better of me, and I wanted Jennifer's help with my decorating plans.

She dried off the last teacup. "I can start right away."

"How about tomorrow." I sighed gratefully. "I don't know what I would do without you and Mark."

As if on cue, Mark arrived with paint chips and wallpaper books, which he plopped down on the table before getting to work measuring the rooms. Not trusting my abilities as a decorator, I showed Jennifer my inspiration folder, and together we picked out a charming pink and green floral wallpaper for the walls, and eggshell paint for the wainscoting and trim.

We agreed Jennifer would start work at ten the next day, but when I told her I'd be baking miniature Victorian sponge cakes, she asked if she could stay and watch.

"I could bake a full-sized one and serve, but the pictures of the mini cakes looked much cuter." I found the picture on my laptop and showed her. She agreed and generously offered to be my taste tester.

Going through the storeroom, I found what I guessed to be a mini-cheesecake pan. Unlike a muffin tin, the sides were vertical so the final result would look like little cakes rather than muffins. After baking the sponges and letting them cool, I sliced them horizontally, layering them with raspberry jam and unsweetened whipped cream, the way they made them in England. A quick dusting of powdered sugar, and they looked good enough to eat.

I made a few test cakes adding a little sugar to the cream so Jennifer and other volunteers could tell me which they liked better. I liked the authenticity of the original recipe, but I knew a lot of Americans liked their desserts sweeter.

Jennifer chose the cake with the sweetened cream as her favorite. "But let me finish both of them to make sure." She grinned. After a few more bites, she said, "I can't tell much of a difference, to be honest."

Surprised by her comment, I decided I needed another opinion. I considered who else to recruit as taste testers. Irma would be working and getting ready to open her restaurant. I called Freddie's office number and told the woman who answered I'd like to speak with Dr. Severs. Expecting her to take a message, I was surprised when I heard Freddie's voice.

"Hi, April. What's up?"

Her friendly, relaxed manner was so different from any doctor I'd ever visited.

"I hoped you'd have time for us to meet, so I can get your advice. I could stop by your office if that's best."

"Are you looking for my advice as a doctor or as the coroner?"

"Neither." I paused for effect. "I'd like you to taste test some Victorian sponge cakes."

She chuckled. "In that case, why don't you stop by my house tonight." She gave me her address and suggested I come by after seven.

After Jennifer left, I went up to my room to change out of my flour-covered tee shirt. When I came back down to the kitchen to retrieve the cakes from the refrigerator, the cakes looked a little sad. The whipped cream hadn't held up. Maybe that was why some recipes called for buttercream icing instead of whipped cream, but that would definitely make them overly sweet.

Opening my laptop, I researched and found several ways to stabilize whipped cream. If I decided to serve the cakes to my guests, gelatin would be the best choice because it would keep the whipped cream firm longest. But it took the longest to prepare, not to mention the fact that I didn't have any unflavored gelatin in my pantry at the moment. Pudding mix was also suggested, and I filed the information away in my mind to try later. For now, I decided to compare whipped cream with dry milk and with powdered sugar and bring one of each for Freddie to try.

Luckily, I had a couple of sponge cakes that I hadn't finished preparing. I prepared two, one with each filling, and packed them up to take to Freddie's.

CHAPTER 18

Driving along Ocean View Drive north toward the lighthouse, I reached Greentree Lane and turned up the dark street. Barely able to read the numbers on the houses, I drove slowly until I found Freddie's address and got out of the car. Freddie's storybook cottage appeared magical in the pale light from a half moon, with ivy climbing up the dark green walls to the steep roofline. I felt miles away from the real world, with the only sound coming from the trees rustling in the wind.

The porchlight came on. As I walked up the stone walkway flanked by spring flowers, I took in all the enchanting details and breathed in the sweet fragrance of night-blooming Jasmine. Before I reached the front door, it opened, and Freddie stepped aside to let me enter.

The inside, as delightful as the exterior, had a bright, clean look, with white walls, cabinets, and tall bookcases. There were so many bookcases, several topped with framed photos. I stopped to admire a picture of a tall, silver-haired man and a stunning, brown-skinned woman who appeared much younger.

"My parents," Freddie said in explanation as I handed her a plastic container with two mini sponge cakes.

"I see you got your high cheekbones from your mother." I took a seat on a slipcovered sofa. "She looks young in that picture," I said, not meaning to be judgmental and hoping it didn't come out that way. "Not that there's anything wrong with that."

She chuckled. "You're not wrong. There's a twenty-year age difference. They met working at the hospital, and the way my father told it, it was love at first sight."

"I don't blame him. She's gorgeous."

"Still is. She moved back to Oakland after he passed away. I'm glad she didn't move back to Haiti. I like having her close."

"Have you been?" I asked.

"To Haiti? A couple of times. I've got some aunties and cousins there. It's always fun to visit—they always try to fatten me up."

I laughed. "That doesn't sound terrible." I'd grown up with few relatives besides my mother and my much older brother. I'd only met an aunt once, before she and my mother had a falling out. Now I only had my brother, but he no longer answered my calls.

I gestured to her bookcases. "I guess you like to read."

Freddie glanced at her collection and grinned. "I've been accused of hoarding books. Every time I think about getting rid of some, I build another bookcase instead." She opened the lid of the container. "These look delicious. I'll get us some plates and forks."

"Those are both for you. There's a slight difference between them, so I'd like to know which one you prefer."

"You're sure?" she asked. "We could share."

"My pants will split if I eat another bite," I said with a laugh. It wasn't far from the truth.

"I won't bother with plates then." She ducked into her little kitchen, calling out, "Would you like a cup of tea? Or perhaps a glass of wine?"

"Wine would be nice." I'd already had about ten cups of tea that day.

She returned, handing me a glass and taking a seat on an overstuffed chair across from me, ready to try the cakes. After tasting both and making happy sounds as she devoured them, she announced she couldn't tell the difference. "What is the difference, anyway?"

I explained my attempt to stabilize the whipped cream. "I might end up using gelatin for them to serve to customers, or maybe a combination. One more decision to make. Lately I can feel my worry lines turning into permanent creases. Only about a thousand more decisions to go."

"It's not a race, you know. Don't forget to enjoy the journey."

I looked at this woman who'd accomplished so much in her young life. "How do you stay so calm? I mean, you have your medical practice, you're the county coroner, and now you're helping with a murder investigation."

"It's a lot," she admitted. "When I start to feel overwhelmed, I take a step back and remind myself why I wanted to become a doctor. Not to get rich or have a cushy life. I wanted to help people the way my dad did."

Financial success aside, I'd accomplished little, unlike Freddie. She'd made a difference. "When you went off to medical school, did you plan on coming back and working with your father?"

She shook her head. "I wanted to move somewhere exciting like L.A. or New York. I did my residency in Baltimore. Boy, talk about culture shock. I decided I wanted to live where people knew me and accepted me."

I hoped she'd bring up the murder investigation, so I

didn't have to. She stood and carried the container to the kitchen. When she returned, my impatience got the better of me.

"Did you learn anything more from the autopsy?" I asked. "I assume you performed one."

She took a sip of her wine and gave me an indulgent smile. "The autopsy results are confidential as part of an ongoing criminal investigation."

I slumped back on the sofa. "I should have realized that." Perhaps I could phrase a question in such a way that she could answer without breaking the rules. Or she might know information besides the autopsy results.

"You look like you're dying to ask me something," Freddie said.

"Guilty," I admitted. "I'm wondering if there's evidence that someone dragged him from the back yard. Like dirt or pebbles in his clothes."

"I can confirm his cause of death was environmental hypothermia exacerbated by his head wound and high intoxication levels."

"Environmental hypothermia? You mean he froze to death, right? That must take a while." I shivered at the thought.

"It would probably take a few hours to succumb to hypothermia, assuming the freezer temperature was zero degrees Fahrenheit or thereabouts. I'd like to think he didn't regain consciousness after he'd been locked in."

I couldn't imagine the terror of waking up inside a locked freezer. "But if he had come to and banged on the door, we might have heard him. We might have been able to save him."

"We'll never know."

∼

THE NEXT MORNING dawned bright and sunny for a change. I sat at the kitchen island with my breakfast of toast and a strong cup of English Breakfast tea with milk. Mark arrived and poked his head into the kitchen. A young man lurked behind him.

"This is Tyler," he said. "He's helping me with the work."

I greeted the young man whose bleached blond hair and tanned arms make me think he must be a surfer. He mumbled shyly in reply.

"We'll get started on the painting," Mark said. "I'll leave the windows open, but you might want to close the door to the kitchen to keep the paint fumes out."

There were advantages to having two sets of stairs to the second floor, one of which meant that I could completely avoid the front room while they worked.

Under Emile's watchful eye, I put the chicken bones I'd purchased in my biggest pot and set it to simmer. After it came to a full boil, I skimmed the surface to remove the foam and fat. I skimmed it a second time and then began adding my vegetables.

"Leave the skins on the onions," he instructed. "They will provide color for the broth."

Making stock didn't require cutting anything into little pieces, so the work went quickly. I cut the onions into four pieces and threw them in the pot. The chef showed me how to wash the leek by slicing it partway. Apparently, leeks liked to hide dirt in their many layers. I tucked a bay leaf in the center of the leek, sprinkled it with thyme, and tied it with string.

"How does that look?" I asked proudly.

"Bravo," he said sarcastically. "You Americans expect a medal every time you don't cut off a finger or set the kitchen on fire."

Feeling disappointed, I tossed the leek in the pot, then added the celery, carrots, and parsley. "Now what?" I asked.

"Now it simmers."

Jennifer arrived on time, and I waved her around to the back door to avoid getting in Mark and Tyler's way. She glanced to her right where the crime scene tape hung like leftover party streamers, giving a little shiver before stepping into the warm kitchen.

The moment she stepped through the door she took a deep breath. "It smells heavenly in here," she said, handing me a baguette, still warm. "You said you've been making lots of soup, and Molly's bakery makes delicious bread, so I brought you a loaf."

"Wonderful! I love soup with fresh bread. I've been meaning to pay the bakery a visit. For tea sandwiches, I like to use really fresh bread and slice it thinly. Most bakeries have slicers that can only cut one thickness." I surveyed the kitchen wondering if I had room for one more gadget. "I could get my own adjustable slicer."

Jennifer laughed and gestured to my counters, which held a professional mixer, food processor, blender, and convection oven. "Sure. Counter space is overrated."

I sent Jennifer to the attic to make an assessment and inventory of the furnishings while I updated my to-do list. "The burgundy Windsor chair belongs to Whisk," I informed her.

"Whisk?"

"The cat. He came with the house." Along with the ghost, I added silently.

She gave me a nod and skipped up the stairs.

She returned half an hour later, grinning. "You have some lovely antiques. I made a list of what I recommend using in the tearoom. I don't recommend using the more valuable and delicate pieces, or I'll have a heart attack anytime someone plops down on a chair. A lot of people don't respect antiques."

I cringed thinking of the sergeant parking his sizable posterior on a Queen Anne chair. I could almost hear the splintering sounds as the chair gave way. "I might want to use the more valuable pieces in the second-floor rooms, but that can wait. Did you see the Irish dresser?"

"That was the first thing that caught my eye." She informed me that repainting it would affect its value and suggested we simply give it a good cleaning. It had a nice rustic, weathered appearance, so I agreed. Two sturdy bookcases didn't have any special value, so we agreed to paint them a soft green and arrange them on either side of the dresser.

I opened my notebook to the page where I'd written my wish list of furniture for the tearoom and handed it to her. "Would you go back up to the attic and check off what we already have? When you're done with that, I could use your advice about where to buy used tables and chairs. I want good quality furniture, but I don't have an unlimited budget."

"There are also some nice reproductions available. I'd go cheap on the tables," she suggested, "since they'll be covered in tablecloths, right?"

"Good point."

While Jennifer got busy, I looked at the next item on my to-do list.

- Solve Bob's murder.

$\mathcal{A}$t noon, I insisted Jennifer take a lunch break with me. As I heated two bowls of Potage Parmentier, we made two lists of items I'd want to purchase. She worked on the first list, titled 'necessary,' which included everything we absolutely needed before opening, from teacups and plates to tables and chairs.

On the second list, 'desirable,' I wrote down more tables and china, along with furnishings for what I called the library, one of the two downstairs bedrooms that still had its walls intact. I hadn't decided what to do with the other, but I didn't need to decide right away. I couldn't wait to decorate it in dark tones befitting an English Manor and fill it with leather chairs and old books.

"Put two chandeliers on the 'necessary' list," I said.

She gave me an indulgent smile. "But are they really necessary?"

"I've already bought them, so they must be."

"I see." She wrote them down. "I suppose that means the Princess Di collectible plates are necessary, too."

"You catch on quickly."

I ladled two bowls of thick steaming soup into bowls and cut thick slices of bread. We'd pulled our stools up to the kitchen island when the doorbell rang. I heard Mark speaking to someone.

Kyla entered the kitchen, looking professional as always in a sleek navy dress and heels. At least I'd put on shoes that morning rather than spending the day in slippers. I invited her to join us for soup, and she pulled up a stool to the island while I ladled another bowlful.

Jennifer stood and carried her dishes to the dishwasher. "I'll get back to work on the list if that's okay."

Kyla took a few spoonfuls of soup and a big bite of bread slathered with butter before muttering under her breath. "Sergeant Five is an idiot, you know."

"Idiot is a strong word," I said. Giving people the benefit of the doubt was a habit of mine. "I agree he might be over his head. Being a small-town cop doesn't necessarily mean you're not qualified to run a murder investigation, but something tells me he's lacking."

"He's already decided you're guilty. Do you care to comment?"

I laughed. "I know better than to make a comment to a reporter." Of course, now that I worked for myself, I didn't have a public relations department to refer her to. I watched Kyla enjoy the soup, wondering what her next move would be.

"I researched your background. Opening a tearoom is quite a change from your former career."

"That's true." I felt a little uncomfortable knowing she'd looked into my past, but I had nothing to hide. I'd worked hard all my life and been lucky enough to hit it big when the company I co-founded went public.

"Why'd you leave the corporate world? It seemed like you had it all."

Back then, I thought I did, engaged to my business partner and best friend. "The partnership fell apart." She didn't need to know the details, that while I'd been flying around the country and the world growing our business, he'd been falling in love with another woman.

"What made you decide to buy this house and open a tearoom?" she asked.

I thought back to the day I first saw this house. Was it only a month ago? "I was possessed."

She raised her eyebrows and waited for me to elaborate.

"Possessed by an idea or a dream I had a long time ago. I ducked into every tearoom I found whenever I had the chance. When you're being served afternoon tea, it's like being wrapped in comfort and safety. The world outside with all its worries and strife sort of slips away."

"Sounds lovely," she said. "I can't wait for you to open it."

"Does that mean you'll stop in for afternoon tea? You might be the only one in this entire town looking forward to coming."

She gave me a knowing smile. "The locals will come around. Eventually. It may take them ten years or so. I hope you have the stamina and savings to stick it out. Or take advantage of tourist season and make enough to last the whole year. That's how the hotel stays in business."

I thought about how my tearoom dream included the fantasy of a warm and welcoming small town who would embrace me into their community. It turned out that was as much a figment of my imagination as the chef in my kitchen.

"I have a proposition for you," Kyla said.

It was my turn to raise my eyebrows. Some reporters, from my experience, learned to manipulate others in order to get the story they wanted, even if that story wasn't the whole story or even truthful. I supposed it wasn't that different from the tools I'd used in my sales career.

I could tell she was waiting for my response. "I'm listening."

"You need information to clear your name and, dare I say it? Stay out of jail."

I nodded, waiting for her to get to her point.

"I need information for my story. I have access to certain information that you don't. And vice versa."

"I see."

"I'm not sure you do." She paced nervously. Or perhaps she was excited. "I want out of this town. I've waited long enough for my big break and I'm done waiting. If I can get the inside scoop and do an exposé on a small-town murder, I think the big city boys would take notice."

"And if they don't?"

She looked over her shoulder as if someone might be listening, then quietly said, "I'm thinking of writing a book."

"I see. A true crime story?"

She leaned closer. "A novel based on this town and all its dirty secrets. The corruption and greed. I've got stories that would curl your hair. I'll put the standard disclaimer, 'any resemblance to people living or dead is entirely coincidental' and all that. But everyone will know it's about Serenity Cove. And with a murder at the center of the story—it can't help but sell."

Kyla seemed like a nice lady, but her ambition worried me. What lengths would she go to in order to further her career? Not murder, certainly, but the way she seemed poised to take advantage of Bob's death made me uncomfortable.

"Who do you think did it?" I asked.

She thought for a moment before answering. "It must have been someone who was at the party that afternoon, don't you agree?"

"Makes sense." I waited for her to continue. I wanted to

find out how much she knew before I gave up any information.

"According to Sergeant Five—Sergeant Rawley, you confronted Bob because you found him upstairs."

I didn't like the direction this was going. "You were at the party, too. At least for part of the evening."

She ignored my comment. "Apparently, that's all the evidence he has against you."

"Except that, as far as we're aware, only Mark and I knew the freezer handle was broken. And where I kept the key."

"Yes, but the key wasn't exactly hidden, was it? And if the killer knew the freezer handle was broken, why would they bother locking it?"

"Mark isn't sure it was locked that morning. He assumed it was, so he didn't try the handle."

She raised her eyebrows but didn't comment. After checking her notes, she continued. "The sergeant questioned Mark. Did either of them give any indication about that interview?"

I shook my head. "He's not sharing his so-called investigation with me, except for the details that incriminate me. What did he say to you?"

"Only that Mark is not a suspect." She paged though her notebook. "In fact, he said, and I quote: 'April May is our only suspect at this time.' What a lazy man."

"Thank goodness for the coroner." The moment I said the words, I regretted it.

Her eyes lit up. "Dr. Severs? What did she have to say?"

"She ruled it a homicide."

"I know about that. The sergeant wasn't happy to hear it either, let me tell you. I wonder why?"

"He wanted to rule it an accident and blame me for negligence." I left out how I had started to wonder if he was out to get me. "I get the feeling there's history between those two. Do you know what's up?"

"Only that Freddie tried to get the sergeant fired."

No wonder they were chilly toward each other. "That could add tension to a relationship."

Kyla put her notebook back in her satchel and stood. "I'm going to ask Mark a few questions, if that's alright with you."

"That's up to him."

NO ONE HAD TOLD me how long my storeroom would stop being a crime scene, so I put in a call to Freddie's office. I asked her when I'd be able to use the room again.

"The sergeant should have let you know. You can remove the tape whenever you want." She offered to give me the number for a company that did crime scene clean ups, but I had already decided to buy a new freezer. I couldn't imagine storing frozen peas in the same space where a dead body had been.

The closest industrial supply house was an hour away. They had online or phone ordering available, but I didn't want to take any chances, so I wrote down the model number and measurements of the old freezer before heading out to visit them in person. I let Mark know I'd be gone for a couple of hours and asked him to lock up if he left before I returned.

Jennifer asked for the rest of the afternoon off, so she could run some personal errands, and I quickly agreed. Until the tearoom opened, I didn't need to hold her to a rigid schedule.

I hit traffic on the way, which gave me time to think about the fact that, according to Kyla, I was Sergeant Rawley's only suspect. I arrived shortly before closing, and after listening to the features and benefits of each model, it all seemed so complicated I considered keeping the old one. Then the memory of Bob's body popped into my head and I knew that wasn't an option. I made a decision, and the grateful salesperson promised it would be delivered a week later.

On the return drive, I called my business lawyer who referred me to a criminal defense attorney. I wasn't going to answer any more of the sergeant's questions without a lawyer present.

I stopped to pick up a few groceries, and when I arrived home, Mark and Tyler had left. When I carried the bags into the kitchen, the now familiar sight of the transparent chef stirring a pot on the stove greeted me. Even though I could see the pot, I knew it only existed in my mind.

"Hello, Chef. What are you cooking today?"

He answered my question with a tart, "Where have you been all this time?"

I almost balked at his nosiness and told him it was none of his business, before I remembered my own subconscious spoke through my imaginary friend. At least, I guessed that's how it worked. "I went to order a new walk-in freezer. When they deliver it in a week or so, they'll cart the old one away. Why? Did you miss me?" I gave him my sweetest smile.

He narrowed his eyes. "I found myself disturbed by footsteps in the attic once again. You must consider doing something about all the people coming and going when you're not in."

Before I considered whether there might be any fact to his claim, I rushed up the back stairs and headed for the attic. The door leading to the attic stairs was ajar. I took my phone out of my pocket and started to dial 9-1-1.

What was I going to tell them? That a ghost told me I had

an intruder? I left the number on the screen but didn't press dial.

Slowly I pushed the door wider and crept up the stairs until I saw Whisk sitting upright on his wingback chair, his whiskers twitching.

"Is someone in here, Whisk?" I whispered.

He moved his head side to side as if shaking his head.

"Good." I climbed the last few steps and put my phone back in my pocket before chuckling at myself for talking to a cat. From what I heard, that wasn't unusual, but when they answered back it was time to worry. When I got back downstairs, I would have to call the doctor back and see what was holding up my referral to the neurosurgeon.

I squeezed around boxes and furniture to reach the area where I'd found the pried-off boards before. There were more loose boards than I remembered, or were there? I scolded myself for not taking pictures when I first found them and got out my phone to snap a few, thinking of the saying about closing the barn door after the cows were gone.

The first person I would have suspected of trespassing would have been Bob, if it weren't for the fact that I'd seen his dead body in my freezer. Who else would be rooting around in my attic? I didn't want to have to wait until I had another break-in to get proof that someone had been in my house, but what other choice did I have?

Back in the kitchen, I shared my concerns with Chef. He made a good sounding board, even better than talking to myself.

"Did you see who the intruder was?" I asked.

"He didn't enter the kitchen," he said stirring a thick sauce. "I can't be traipsing around the house after intruders. I have a béchamel to make."

"Fine." As if his béchamel was more important than an

intruder. What was the point of having a ghost in your house if he couldn't scare people off? Thank goodness I had Whisk.

My words to Kyla came back to me. Mark and I were the only two who knew where we'd put the key. On the other hand, the key wasn't exactly hidden. Anyone could have unlocked the freezer and put Bob inside, as long as they were strong enough to drag his body up the steps and into the freezer.

Mark and Tyler had been the only ones in the house while I was out shopping, and Mark had locked up when he left. Did he take advantage of Jennifer's and my absence to search the attic? Did he know what Bob had been looking for in my house?

My not-so-friendly chef must have finished making his sauce, because when I returned to the kitchen he was gone. Good. I didn't want him looking over my shoulder while I made shortbread cookies.

I learned to make shortbread at the age of eight. My mother, who baked wonderful treats on her good days, got tired of me nagging her for cookies. She pulled the flour and sugar down from the cupboard, handed me a stick of butter and a recipe, and told me if I could read, I could bake.

When I got older, I tried other recipes, but nothing comforted me like freshly baked shortbread. I baked a couple of dozen and thought about what to do while drinking tea and taste testing cookies. By the time I'd eaten half of them, I had a plan.

CHAPTER 20

*I*t wasn't hard to get the word out that I would be away from the house on Friday. I called the police station and told Pauline I had to go to the city to meet with my lawyer in case Sergeant Rawley needed to speak with me.

I knew Pauline would tell half the town. When Mark arrived, I asked him if he would mind taking a three-day weekend.

He grinned. "I don't mind at all. I should finish up with the wallpapering by then."

"Great. Let's meet Monday morning and talk about what's next on the plan. I'm driving down to San Francisco around ten, and I'll be gone most of the day." I felt guilty, as if trying to snare him in my trap. But if he weren't involved in the murder or the break-ins, he had nothing to worry about.

That evening, at the Mermaid Cafe, I announced my plans to Irma loud enough for anyone to hear.

When Friday morning arrived, I dressed in slacks and a blazer, so anyone who saw me leave would think I was headed for a business meeting. My binoculars were in my briefcase along with a bag of trail mix.

I drove several blocks away before turning down an alleyway and parking. Fifteen minutes later, I squeezed through my back gate and hid in the bushes. The burglar would be reckless to enter through the front where a passerby might see him or her, so I trained my binoculars on the back door. I didn't have to wait long.

My heart pounded as a figure entered the back gate and slank along the bushes. With the hood of his or her sweatshirt pulled up over their head, I couldn't tell if it was Mark or not. I was pretty sure it was a man, based on his size and build, and I watched as he pushed open a window and climbed in. I hadn't left any of the windows unlocked, but I hadn't checked them in several days. Mark had plenty of opportunities to unlatch a window, but I didn't want to believe it was him.

I called the police station, telling Pauline I had an intruder.

"Are you sure?" she said.

"Yes," I whispered. "I'm in my back yard and I just watched him go in one of the windows."

"Don't you lock them?"

"Yes, I locked them. Someone must have opened one when they were in the house."

"I thought you went to see your lawyer today. What are you doing in your back yard?"

I didn't have time for this. "Would you send Sergeant Rawley over right away?" I heard my voice rise in frustration.

"Okay, okay, you don't need to get testy about it."

I took a deep breath, and in what I hoped was a calm, pleasant voice, repeated my request. "Please ask him to stop by as soon as he can."

Making my way to the front of the house, I waited impatiently for the sergeant's patrol car. When he finally arrived, I waved him over and told him about what I'd seen.

"I think he might be in my attic. There's evidence some-one's been up there looking for something."

Sergeant Rawley scowled. "You better not be making all this up to throw suspicion on someone else. There are laws against making frivolous calls."

I unlocked the front door, and we entered the parlor. "I'm going into the kitchen to watch the back staircase." Darned if I was going to let my intruder slip out the back while Rawley went up the front.

I listened to his footsteps going up the stairs to the second floor. I wondered if the intruder heard them too, or if he was too engrossed in prying panels off my attic wall to notice.

After several minutes, I heard the sergeant's plodding steps overhead, and he called out to someone. I waited expectantly to see who came down the steps, wondering if I should have let the out-of-shape cop go up there alone.

When clomping feet came down the stairs, I dashed into the front room in time to see Harold heading my way with Sergeant Rawley prodding him forward.

"Stop shoving me," Harold said. "I'd promised April to find a new home for the cat. I've been up there trying to round him up for the past half hour."

The Sergeant looked at me. "Did you ask Mr. Perrino to find a new home for your cat?"

"Yes, but that was weeks ago, and he told me I should keep him as a mouser." I put my hands on my hips. "And that doesn't explain why he would come into my house without my permission after I had the locks changed or why he climbed through the window."

Harold knew he was caught in a lie, but he wasn't about to admit it. "I wanted to surprise you."

"Balderdash," came from the doorway of the kitchen, and I turned to see Chef standing there glowering.

"I know," I said to him.

"You know what?" Sergeant Rawley said.

"I know that Harold has been looking for something in my attic. Something hidden."

"That's ridiculous." Harold lifted his chin imperiously as if he would never stoop to such a thing. "You make it sound like I'm looking for treasure or something." He rubbed his hands together like a villain from a melodrama. "Ooh, maybe I have a treasure map. Did pirates bury treasure in your attic?"

The Sergeant looked at Harold, as if deciding whose side he wanted to be on. He turned to me. "Do you have proof?"

"Wait here." I dashed up the stairs. This time I could tell there were several more boards pulled out than before. What was Harold looking for?

I took pictures of the damage and came back down the stairs. I walked right up to Harold. "I have pictures of the boards from yesterday morning and pictures from now. If you didn't pry those boards off the wall, who did? The cat?"

"Yowrr."

I turned to see Whisk at the top of the stairs. He narrowed his eyes at me as if I was actually accusing him.

"I don't know what you're talking about," Harold said. "I told you I came here to get the cat. You claimed to be deadly allergic to it, but I've never seen you so much as sneeze."

"The doctor says I've outgrown the allergy, and as it happens, I've grown rather fond of Whisk." He almost made me lose my train of thought. "Don't change the subject. I caught Bob upstairs the day he died. Was he looking for something too? What was it?"

"I remember that day," Harold said. "You exchanged words with him, if I recall."

"Yes, funny thing. I don't like people creeping around my house without my permission."

135

The Sergeant interrupted my rant. "Are you planning to press charges?"

I ignored him. "Bob was looking for something in my house and now you are. Bob lived here as a child, and maybe he told you about treasure hidden in the walls. Is that why you killed him, Harold?"

Sergeant Rawley gasped. "You can't go around accusing people of murder, Ms. May."

"Is that so? You accused me, without any proof, without any motive. At least Harold has a motive. With Bob gone, he can have the treasure to himself." It sounded like a good theory to me.

The Sergeant cleared his throat. "Except that Mr. Perrino has an alibi for the time of the murder."

"Baloney," I said, on a roll now. "No one knows what time Bob was dragged into the freezer. How can he have an alibi?"

The Sergeant's face reddened. "Mr. Perrino has an alibi from the time Bob Shimp was last seen alive until the following morning. Now, unless you want to press charges, I think we're done here."

"I DON'T BUY IT," I said to Chef as I rolled out pie crust for Quiche Lorraine. I'd found the recipe in one of his books, and it occurred to me that mini quiches would be perfect for afternoon tea. My first attempt would be a full-sized quiche. If it came out well, I'd look into buying small tart tins and testing the recipe on a smaller scale. Or perhaps I could make them in a muffin tin.

I continued thinking aloud while I worked. "Harold has to be the murderer. I always thought he had shifty eyes. His so-called-alibi has to be a fake."

"Don't sprinkle so much flour on your crust or your

result will be as tough as an overcooked rump roast." He added, "I recall you stating he seemed like a nice fellow."

"Yes. A nice fellow with shifty eyes."

"Your dough is too warm," he scolded. "Put it back in the refrigerator for fifteen minutes or so."

"Fine." When I returned to the kitchen, I asked, "Now what?"

He looked down his nose at me but said nothing. I would have thrown my rolling pin at him if it weren't for the fact it would go right through him. I'd have to settle for verbal sparring. "I'm not sure what good you are if you're not going to tell me what to do."

I set a skillet on the stove and laid a single slice of bacon in it, turning the fire up to medium high.

"There," he said, smirking. "I knew you could figure it out. You may slice the onion while you wait for the bacon to crisp. Of course, if you were my sous chef, I would expect you to have all the ingredients prepped and ready before you commenced cooking."

"Uh-huh." I only half listened to his lecture. "I wonder who would know about Harold's alibi." In my mind, I went through the list of the few people I knew in town. "I know, I'll call Kyla." I stepped into the other room to make the phone call.

It turned out Kyla knew about the alibi. She repeated the details I'd gotten from Sergeant Rawley, saying Harold left the house at four, at the same time as Bob.

"Yeah, I know that part," I said impatiently.

"Then he met with some clients in Somerton twenty minutes away. He arrived there at around twenty minutes after."

"Or so he says," I interjected.

"Or so his clients say. I wasn't going to take Harold's word for it either, so I called them. They're an older couple, looking to downsize. The wife told me that Harold was already waiting for them when they arrived and when they entered the house it was twenty-four minutes after four."

"That's very specific," I said. "A little too specific."

"I hear what you're saying," Kyla said, "but she was very insistent."

"Okay, but what about the rest of the day? How does someone have an alibi for an entire evening and night?"

"He was with his clients until shortly after five when he went to a nearby restaurant. After dinner, he went into the bar where he had drinks with a woman friend. Apparently, he spent the rest of the evening and night with her."

"She's lying."

"Doesn't matter, unless you think the murder happened after midnight because that's when he left the bar. According to the coroner, time of death was sometime before nine p.m. She can't narrow it down any further, not knowing what time he ended up in the freezer."

"Thanks," I said and hung up the phone. Thanks for nothing.

CHAPTER 21

*E*mile had a hissy fit when I returned to the kitchen.

"What are you thinking? Notwithstanding the fact that you have begun the quiche without the necessary preparations, now you are leaving the bacon unattended."

"Cool your jets." I began to miss the peace and quiet of a chef-free kitchen. "The bacon is fine. See?" I picked it up with my fork to show him.

"You might at the very least use the proper tools," he huffed. "Where have you hidden my tongs?"

"They must be here somewhere." I opened several drawers until I found a pair, and then I removed the bacon from the skillet and placed it on paper towels.

"Surely you must have cheesecloth at your disposal," he huffed.

"Didn't you have paper towels when you were alive?"

He shot daggers at me with his eyes. "I am not a common housewife."

While I sautéed the onion, I only half listened to Emile's chatter. I couldn't shake the idea that Harold must have murdered Bob in spite of his so-called iron-clad alibi. I didn't buy his story about coming to get Whisk for a second. Even if he wasn't a murderer, he might be taking advantage of Bob's death to keep the treasure for himself, whatever it was. "Treasure," I muttered. I had to admit it sounded ridiculous. Still, there were a number of items of value in the house, such as the antique furniture.

I hadn't looked through the books yet to see if any were first editions, but something told me neither Bob nor Harold had been looking for a rare book.

"There must be something in this house. But what?" I wondered aloud, glancing at Chef to see if he had any opinions. "It must be something hidden here when Bob was growing up."

"Are you planning to incinerate the onion?" he asked, his voice dripping with sarcasm.

I turned the burner off, crumbled the bacon into the pie crust, and added the onions. "Didn't Bob's mother die when he was off at college?"

"I can't say I recall."

Of course, that was long after he left town. Perhaps if I repeated the stories Irma had told me about Norma, he'd remember something. I'd worry later about the fact I was beginning to think my apparition was a real ghost. "Norma and Barbara both lived here—Norma upstairs and Barbara downstairs."

Chef Emile appeared completely uninterested in my walk down memory lane. "The cheese will not cube itself, in case you supposed it might."

I grabbed the block of cheese and started chopping. "That was before Norma hired you, wasn't it? What did you do before you came to Serenity Cove?" Perhaps a direct question would get him to open up.

"I gained my culinary knowledge at the side of the most skilled chefs in Paris. Once I had learned all they could teach me, I came to this country and became the chef du cuisine at Maison Brisson." He stated the last fact proudly, obviously expecting me to be impressed.

"Maison Brisson? In Beverly Hills?" I'd heard of it, but I didn't have the heart to tell him it closed years ago.

"*Mais ouis*. All the movie stars dined at my restaurant, some quite frequently. They lingered over cognac and cordials hoping I would visit their tables and accept their praise."

"Then how'd you end up in this out of the way place?"

"Norma Thornly had a certain *je ne sais quoi*. She recognized my skill and savvy the way no other had before." He sighed, lost in the memory. "She lured me away, imploring me to come here to establish a restaurant the likes of which had never been seen before."

"She offered you more money?"

He scoffed. "Money. This is all you Americans think about. What she offered me, money could not buy. Complete control over the menu and never a question about how I spent the funds allotted me. And the *piece de resistance*, she promised to hire an assistant to prepare my cookbooks for publication. I found her offer too tempting to resist."

"And you were falling in love with Norma?"

He didn't expect that, but quickly regained his composure. "It was hard not to fall in love with Norma. Nearly every man who came into her orbit found themselves smitten with her. But I didn't have any illusions that we would be a couple. I was content to be her business partner. "

"So, with you as the chef and Norma as the glamorous and charming proprietor, the restaurant was a big success."

Chef gazed into the other room; his eyes locked on the staircase. "When Norma came down the stairs in her gown and her jewels, it was a glorious sight to see."

"That's it! Her jewels." Were Norma's jewels hidden in the

house? You certainly wouldn't leave them lying around where a burglar could steal them, especially when you shared your home with your business. "How did Norma die? Was it sudden?"

"How would I know?" His voice softened, and he stared out the window.

Silly me. As a figment of my imagination, he couldn't know anything I didn't know. I put the cubed cheese in the pie and returned to the cookbook to check the next step.

"After all, I died long before she did." I heard a deep sadness in his voice.

Did his sadness come from his unrequited love or because he was dead? If he hadn't died then, he'd surely be dead by now. I couldn't keep my mind off the jewels. It made so much sense. If they were hidden in the walls as Harold seemed to think, I would have to figure out the best way to find them. A metal detector, perhaps? I considered asking Mark, but now that I knew Harold had an alibi, Mark was the most likely suspect.

Darn. I liked Mark.

Mark was the only one besides me who knew the freezer handle was broken, and he knew where I'd put the keys. But why would he kill Bob?

IF I WEREN'T LOOKING for information, I wouldn't go back to the Mermaid Cafe anytime soon. Or ever. You'd think I'd get used to people staring at me, like I was some sort of infamous internet star. Being the focus of local gossip offered its own type of celebrity.

As I walked to my table, I nodded to the well-heeled patrons in the booth on the right who averted their gazes.

The riffraff at the bar had no problem staring right back at me.

"Special today is corned beef and cabbage," Irma said.

I couldn't remember the last time I'd had corned beef, but I was still distracted by the stares. I tilted my head toward the booths. "You'd think they'd get used to having an accused murderer in their midst by now."

"Yes, but now you're an accused murderer who slandered one of our long-time citizens. That's much worse than murder."

She had the hint of a smile, but I suspected she didn't want to be seen carrying on a long conversation with me, so I ordered the corned beef. "I'll take a whiskey, too. Irish whiskey if you have it."

When she returned with my whiskey, I said, "Can I ask you something?"

She narrowed her eyes at me but said nothing, which I took as assent.

"How did Norma die? Was it sudden?"

"Norma? Why are you asking about her? Don't tell me you're writing a book, too."

"No, why? Who's writing a book?" Kyla had said she planned to write a novel, but I didn't believe her one hundred percent. I told myself to focus. "I'm not writing a book. I'm trying to stay out of jail. Do you remember what happened to Norma?"

"She fell down the stairs and broke her neck." She pulled out a chair and sat down, as if she were enjoying giving me the details. "Died instantly, according to her doctor."

"Was she old or ill?"

"In her early fifties and healthy as a horse," she informed me with a hint of a smile. "There were rumors she'd been pushed, but they couldn't prove anything."

Was this a clue? My gut told me there was a connection

with Bob's death. Or her death might have been connected to the jewels hidden in my house. "Who did people think pushed her?"

"Well, the only other person in the house at the time was her sister Barbara. She'd moved back in after her husband died."

"Where was Bob?"

"Away at college. When he returned, his aunt wouldn't let him into the house. She packed up his and Norma's belongings and stored them in the garage for him."

"And Bob's father?"

"You ask an awful lot of questions." Irma turned to walk away.

"Wait! Do you know someone who has a metal detector?"

Irma stopped and eyed me curiously. "Perhaps."

"I'd like to borrow one for a couple of days. I might be totally off track, but I think it might help me solve the murder. Or at least confirm the motive. That's a start, right?"

Irma hesitated before nodding. "I have one. I'll bring it over tomorrow as long as you explain why you need one."

I took a quick look around to make sure no one was within earshot. In a quiet voice, I said, "I'm looking for hidden jewels."

Her eyes widened. "I'll be there first thing in the morning."

After dinner, I walked the short distance home. Maybe I shouldn't walk after dark but looking up at the starry sky while being soothed by the sounds of the crashing waves, I felt safe. After all, Bob's murder wasn't some random act of violence. As long as the murderer didn't decide to come after me, I should be fine. What if the murderer found out I was onto him? What if he were willing to kill for the jewels—the jewels that might still be hidden in my home?

If Norma had hidden her jewelry in the house, surely

Barbara or Bob would have known about it and not left them there. But perhaps, being relatively young, she'd thought she had plenty of time to tell her son or didn't know whom she could trust. The thought her own sister might have pushed her down the stairs disturbed me, even if it was decades ago.

Whether Norma told Bob or not, he must have known. Perhaps she'd told him when he was a child, or he'd followed her and seen her hide them. He might have been waiting for decades for his aunt to pass away assuming she would leave him the house. Sometimes things don't work out the way you expect.

CHAPTER 22

I didn't see any point in setting the alarm when I went to bed. Saturday morning, I woke begrudgingly. I began to lose hope my tearoom would ever open. Finally, hunger lured me downstairs, where I put the kettle on and searched through the cupboards for something quick to make.

Chef Emile observed me as I popped a couple of pieces of bread in the toaster. "I see you're opting for a gourmet breakfast today."

"That reminds me. I need to call and get that referral." I pushed the lever on the toaster down, or rather I tried. It kept popping back up.

"Referral?" he asked. "What would that be regarding?"

I checked the plug, then pushed the toaster lever again. No luck. "For the neurosurgeon, so I'll quit having these hallucinations." I started to explain in more detail before muttering to myself, "Why am I having this conversation with him?"

He straightened up and gave me a haughty look. "Because no one else wants to listen to you prattle on, perhaps? As for me, I don't seem to have any choice in the matter."

I put the stale bread on a plate and stared at it. Wanting to cry but realizing it would be stupid to shed tears over a broken toaster, I turned to Emile. "Okay, Mr. Genius Chef. What should I do with two pieces of bread and a broken toaster?"

"Ah, oui." Suddenly, I had his full attention. "Pain perdu!"

"Pamperdoo?"

He gave his head a little shake as I reached for the cookbook. "Which volume is it in?"

"To prepare Pain perdu," he spoke slowly, as if I were a child, "One dips bread in a mixture of eggs and milk among other ingredients. Then it is fried and dusted with icing sugar."

"You mean French toast."

"Sacre bleu," he exclaimed. "I will show you how to make Chef Emile's Pain Perdu. When you take the first bite, then you may tell me it is 'French Toast.'" He said 'French toast' in an exaggerated American accent, which made me giggle, and I caught him smile ever so briefly.

I flipped through *Modern French Cooking*. "Which book is it in?"

"Leave those be. The recipe is in here." He pointed to his forehead or possibly the brim of his chef's hat.

I stopped myself from asking if he had a rat in his hat, since I assumed he hadn't seen any animated films in the last several decades. "Okay, but you said, 'icing sugar,' and I don't want to run to the store right now. I'm hungry."

"You Americans call it powdery sugar."

"Powdered sugar?"

"That is what I said. Do you have an orange?" He paused for me to nod. "Cointreau?"

"Huh?"

He pursed his lips in apparent frustration. "Orange liqueur."

I left the room and returned with a bottle. Doing my best to follow directions, after thoroughly washing the orange, I grated the outside of it vigorously.

He chastised me. "We only want the very outside of the skin. The pith will add a bitter taste to the dish."

"Got it."

Next, I squeezed half the juice into the bowl and added in a splash of orange liqueur along with the zest. Then I added two eggs, sugar, milk, and a splash of cream and whisked it gently.

"Now you may whisk briskly." He watched me for a few moments. "Yes, that should do it."

"Should?" I'd never known anyone who had recipes stored in their mind. What if he left out a critical ingredient?

After dipping the bread in the mixture and putting it the oven, I waited expectantly to taste the final results. I plated the Pain Perdu and sprinkled it with powdered sugar. Emile watched me as I took the first bite.

"Mmm…" I'd found my new favorite breakfast dish.

After I'd washed the dishes, I poured a cup of tea, pulled a stool over to the island, and wondered what to do with myself all day. I went through my to-do list, but I felt uninspired. All my motivation had evaporated along with my excitement.

A text from Jennifer came through saying she wasn't sure when she could come back to work. She didn't seem the type who would let rumors bother her, but maybe I'd misjudged her. Did I seem more guilty to the townspeople since I had accused Harold? It was just the sort of thing a guilty person would do.

I'd never meant to come to this town, even for one night, but I ended up falling in love with it and staying. Had I fallen in love with a mirage? It had been an impractical decision to buy this house. Why had I done it?

I'd bought this house because it felt like home. It still did, but the town didn't. What was I going to do now?

"Are you ready to get to work?" Chef asked.

I stared at him. "I just finished cleaning the kitchen. Besides, I'm busy."

"It seems you are busy staring at the walls. There is much for you to learn and feeling sorry for yourself is not in the least productive."

"I wasn't feeling sorry—okay maybe I was, a little." I gulped the last of my tea and put my cup in the sink. "It's not my fault I can't open the shop. I'm waiting on several permits and my freezer is a crime scene."

He looked up at the ceiling as if looking for divine assistance, then looked me straight in the eye. "You need to learn how to make the other mother sauces. It's the most important technique for a French chef to perfect. We shall start with a Velouté."

I wondered if I'd heard him right. "Mother sauces?"

He sighed. "There are five mother sauces. You have made a béchamel. The others are Sauce Tomat, Hollandaise, Espagnole, and Velouté."

"And why are they called mother sauces?"

He gave me one of his condescending smiles. "Because once you can prepare all five mother sauces, there are no limits to the sauces you can create. With a Velouté, you may prepare a white wine sauce or a sauce Allemande, par exemple."

"So, do you call them daughter sauces?" I guessed, waiting for him to correct me or insult me or possibly both.

"They are." He stared at me, waiting for me to capitulate.

"Fine." What else was I going to do all day? I pulled my

apron over my head. "Let's get cooking. Can we start with the white wine sauce?"

～

A TAPPING on the back door startled me. I found Jennifer on the back steps with the hood of her jacket over her head. "My dad thinks I'm going to my other job."

I invited her to join me in the kitchen. "I don't want to get you in trouble with him."

"One of these days, he has to accept I'm a grown woman. Who were you talking to?"

"What?" I glanced at Chef and back to her. "I was talking to myself. I do that a lot, now that I live alone. And the cat. I talk to the cat all the time."

"I talk to the antiques," she admitted shyly. "Of course, they don't talk to me. That would be crazy, right? I wish they could. Think of what they could tell us. I mean you can read about the old times, but it's not the same, is it?"

"Nope." Not like having a fifty's chef to tell you all about the good old days when women knew their places. I invited her to pull a stool up to the island and poured her a cup of tea. "Sorry, I still don't know how to work the cappuccino machine."

She hopped off her stool. "I bet I can figure it out for you. I used to be a barista when we had a coffee house in town." She began inspecting the machine.

"A coffee house can't even stay in business in this town?" What hope did I have with my tearoom?

"The place burned down, and the owner moved back to Florida instead of rebuilding." She lowered her voice. "Very suspicious circumstances, if you ask me. Do you have espresso?"

Jennifer poured water into the machine, filled a

doohickey with coffee, and turned a few dials. She gave me a nervous smile, said, "Here goes nothing," and flipped a switch.

The machine started to hiss, and a few moments later, dark liquid resembling coffee came out of the spigot.

I jumped off my stool and gave her a high five.

"Americano, latte, or cappuccino?" she asked.

Jennifer made us frothy cappuccinos while I reheated a few slices of Pain Perdu.

"By the way," I said, "all the cappuccinos you can drink is a perk of the job."

"Oh boy. You'd better stock up on decaf. You don't want to see me after ten cappuccinos." She grinned, but then her smile faded. "I heard about the whole thing with Harold Perrino and how you accused him of murdering Bob."

"Great. I guess the whole town must know. Did you hear he broke into my house?"

Her eyes widened. "No kidding? You'd think my dad would have mentioned that part."

"I think I'm supposed to be the villain in this story, and that little tidbit didn't support the narrative."

Jennifer blinked. "Huh?"

"Never mind."

I heard another tapping. I went to the back door and opened it wide enough to see Irma holding a metal detector.

"What's the password?" I whispered.

"What are you talking about? Let me in before someone sees me."

"I thought someone had turned my house into a speakeasy while I slept. I understand Jennifer sneaking in the back way, but who are you hiding from, Irma?"

"Everyone." She leaned the metal detector against the side of the island and took a stool, while watching Jennifer make her a cappuccino. "If my regulars find out I'm talking to you, they won't leave me alone. I keep telling them I'm not the town gossip, but they complain that Pauline's information isn't accurate."

I laughed, and she gave me a startled look before she started chuckling too.

Jennifer shook her head. "It's not fair. Does anyone really think April locked Bob in her freezer? I mean, how did she get him in there? Lure him with cheese puffs?"

"They were really good cheese puffs," Irma said.

I wished I knew who I could trust. Did these two not know the details about how Bob died? I waited to see how Irma would respond.

"He was hit over the head," she said, "then dragged in there."

Jennifer gasped. "No way."

"Way," Irma said. "Can you see April here dragging a 160-pound man for more than a foot? It's ridiculous. I would have accused Harold too. Too bad he has an alibi."

"Practically iron-clad," I said, getting up to get another piece of Pain Perdu and one for Irma. "But if he didn't do it, then who?"

Irma watched me until I sat down again. "You have someone in mind."

"No," I said. "Well, maybe. I mean I don't want to think—"

"Spit it out," she said.

"The only one besides me who knew the handle was broken was Mark. And he knew where the key was. Of course, he has absolutely no motive, so that brings us back to square one."

Irma and Jennifer glanced at each other.

"What are you two not telling me?" I asked.

Jennifer motioned to Irma to go first.

"You know about Mark's son."

I nodded. "Mark said he returned to town when his ex-wife remarried and moved out of town, so his son didn't have to change schools."

"William," Jennifer said, staring at her coffee cup. "His name was William."

"Was?" Why was she talking about him in the past tense?

"William went to school with me in Somerton. There are so few kids here, they bussed us to other schools. We were in our senior year."

I didn't like the way this story was going.

"You tell her the rest," Jennifer said to Irma, not lifting her eyes.

Irma patted Jennifer's arm and turned back to me. "Dr. Severs gave William a prescription, and Mark had it filled at Bob's pharmacy, of course. But he gave him the wrong medication."

"Is that bad?" I asked.

"In this case, it probably wouldn't have been a problem, but William had a heart murmur. It was undiagnosed, which is fairly common. After his death, Doc got suspicious, and being the coroner, she did a tox screen. Then she got the prescription bottle from Mark and found out about the mix-up."

"Why is he still allowed to prescribe medication?" I asked.

"He wasn't for quite a while. He hired a pharmacist to work for him for a few years until he had his license reinstated."

Another knock on the back door. I looked at Irma and Jennifer, but they both shrugged.

Opening the door a crack to make sure it wasn't Jennifer's dad or all the regulars from the Mermaid cafe, I recognized Freddie's curls. I threw the door open and invited her in.

"Hi. I hope I'm not interrupting."

"Actually, we were just talking about you." I explained I'd learned about Mark's son's death and the details surrounding it. I needed to stretch my legs, so I gave Freddie my stool and Jennifer showed me how to draw a shot of espresso.

"How's Sergeant Five doing with the investigation?" Irma asked the doctor.

Freddie grimaced, obviously wanting to get something off her chest. "I have the utmost respect for law enforcement. Many of them put their lives on the line to uphold the law and protect citizens. But our acting Police Chief…" her voice trailed off.

"Is over his head," I said, completing her thought. It seemed the most diplomatic way to put it. "Murder investigations take special skills, and I don't think Rawley is the right man for the job."

"You're not saying we should go behind his back and call the sheriff's office, I hope." Freddie shuddered. "You do that, and the place will be overrun with overzealous deputies."

"I'm saying we have to solve the murder and hand Sergeant Five—" I suppressed a grin. "Now you have me doing it. If we turn over all the evidence proving who killed Bob, and we let him take all the credit, then things around here can go back to normal."

"I don't know why everyone in town doesn't like you," Freddie said.

CHAPTER 23

Freddie asked for some paper, and I grabbed a small notebook from the junk drawer. She handed it back to me.

"You can take notes," she said.

"Why me?" I whined.

Irma gave me a pen. "You have the most at stake here, so put on your big girl panties, and start writing. You might want to start with a list of everyone at the party."

That was easy. I said each name as I wrote it down. "Bob, Mark, you-Irma, you-Jennifer, Harold."

"Don't forget Kyla," Freddie said. "I would think she'd be one of the top suspects."

"Why do you say that?" I asked.

"Because she used to be married to Bob."

"Excuse me?" I stopped writing and looked up. The three women nodded. "Why didn't anyone think to mention that sooner?"

Irma shrugged. "I assumed you knew. You seemed to be buddy-buddy with her."

I wrote Kyla's name in big letters and put a big star next to it. Then I circled it and underlined it. "Tell me everything."

Irma explained that Kyla and Bob married about ten years earlier. Kyla wanted to pursue a journalism career, and Bob paid for her schooling as well as a makeover and an entire new professional wardrobe.

Freddie interrupted her. "You make it sound like she took advantage of him or married him for his money. It wasn't like that at all."

Irma continued. "Bob was head over heels in love with Kyla. When the money started to run out, he took out a second mortgage on his house. Anything to avoid telling Kyla they couldn't afford the lifestyle they were living."

"And Kyla had no clue?"

"I don't think she did," Irma said. "And then she got a bad rap because when the money ran out, she left him. Everyone thinks it's because he was broke, but it was actually because he lied to her."

I didn't blame her one bit. "That is so wrong—to mortgage their house and not tell her. So how long have they been divorced?"

"It's been four or five years," Irma said. "But Bob never gave up trying to get her back."

"No wonder he's been trying to find the hidden jewels," I said absentmindedly.

Everyone turned to stare at me. I told them about my theory that Norma had hidden her jewelry in the house. "Somehow Harold must have found out about it, so he took over the search. That's why I was so sure he killed Bob."

Freddie stood up and slammed her hand on the island startling the three of us. "That explains it."

Jennifer, Irma and I stared at her.

"I found a single diamond and ruby earring in Bob's pocket," Freddie said. "I couldn't figure it out, but what if that's why he was murdered? Maybe there was more in his pockets, but the killer inadvertently left behind an earring."

This was the big breakthrough we'd been waiting for. "If we find the other earring, we find the killer."

"That sounds great," Irma said, "but who's going to go into Kyla's home and search for an earring?"

I raised my hand.

"No, no, no," Freddie said, shaking her head. "Bad idea."

"You said it yourself. I'm the one with the most at stake."

"You're also the one who will look guilty if you're caught breaking into someone's house."

Jennifer piped up. "And if you find something, the police will probably think you planted it there to make her look guilty."

I deflated. "You have a point."

"Wait a second" Irma said. "Is Kyla our only suspect, then?"

I stared at one name on the paper and clicked the pen repeatedly. I didn't want to say what I was thinking out loud.

Freddie grabbed the pen out of my hand. "Well?"

"It's just…" I started, took a deep breath and started again. "I don't even want to think it, much less say it out loud."

"Mark." Freddie said. "It's so hard to believe."

Jennifer shook her head violently. "It's not hard at all. Bob killed William."

The three women talked over each other until I interrupted with a loud whistle. I turned to Freddie. "I think we have to admit it. Mark might have killed Bob."

The doorbell rang, so I left the trio in the kitchen. Before I reached the front door, the visitor began banging impatiently.

"I'm coming," I called out. "Keep your shorts on."

I saw Jennifer's father through the glass and slowed my pace, calling out loudly, "Hello, Mr. Skillings." I hoped

Jennifer heard me and got the hint. I opened the door, and he pushed past me.

"Where is she? I know she's here." He made it to the kitchen before I could stop him, and I prepared myself for a family altercation.

Jennifer must have slipped out the back, thank goodness, and someone had cleared away the extra coffee cup.

"Hello, Mr. Skillings," Freddie said.

"Where is she?" He stepped into the storeroom but stopped when he saw the crime scene tape. Taking a few steps backward, he turned to Freddie. "Is that where Bob...?"

Freddie nodded. "Jennifer's not here, sir. Have you tried calling her?"

He shook his head. "She's not answering."

Freddie reached for his arm, but he pulled back. "Jennifer's a good girl. You can trust her."

He narrowed his eyes, glancing at Irma and back to Freddie. "You don't know the half of it. I have to keep her safe. You don't know what we've been through."

Irma spoke up. "We know plenty. Jennifer is a grown woman, and if you don't start treating her like one, you're going to lose her."

"She's my daughter," he said, his voice rising. "You stay out of it. And you," he pointed at me, "Stay away from her."

Before I could respond, Freddie took his arm. He shook her off, and she followed him to the front door. They spoke briefly, but I couldn't hear the words.

"What was that about?" I asked Irma. "Why does he have such a grudge against me?"

"Pretty much everyone in town thinks you killed Bob."

My mouth dropped open. "They do? But there's no proof."

"A good rumor is way more convincing than proof."

I sighed. "I've got to find out the truth and clear my name."

Irma nodded. "All we need to do is find the other earring. We need to search their homes."

It didn't sound like a wise plan, but I wasn't sure we had a better one. I nodded as Freddie returned to the room.

She took one look at us and said, "What are you two up to?"

"Nothing." I did my best to appear innocent. "Why is Jennifer's father so overprotective of her? She's a grown woman, but he treats her like a child."

Irma glanced at Freddie before speaking. "In her second year of college, her mother was driving her back to school when their car went off the side of the road and crashed."

"My goodness, was she hurt?" I asked.

"Yes, I heard she was in a coma for several days," Freddie said. "My dad told me it was touch and go for a while there. That was before I moved back to town."

"There's more," Irma said quietly.

Freddie took over the story. "Her mother didn't make it. Her dad's personality completely changed. He never had what you would call a sunny disposition, but he became almost paranoid. Hardly wanted to let Jennifer out of his sight."

"I actually don't blame him," I admitted.

"I've got to get going," Freddie said, carrying her cup to the sink.

"Good," Irma replied. "We've got work to do."

Freddie raised her eyebrows but said nothing, obviously used to Irma's blunt manner. When I returned from showing her out, Irma picked up the metal detector and headed up the stairs.

"Wait," I said. "I'm hungry." When she gave me a disappointed look, I told her it would only take a few minutes to heat us up some soup.

"Potage Parmentier?" she asked hopefully.

After lunch, I left the dishes in the sink and followed her upstairs. An hour later, we'd found every nail in the attic walls, but nothing else. Then we focused on the furniture, and the metal detector pinged at each hinge and handle. Not willing to give up, I started at one end of the attic, waving it over boxes and chairs until my arms ached.

Finally, I admitted my plan was a bust. "Maybe there wasn't anything other than the necklace and earrings Bob found."

"Or there could be diamonds and rubies that aren't set in gold or platinum," Irma suggested. When I shook my head at her unlikely scenario, she visibly deflated. "You're right. I guess our treasure hunt is over."

"Thanks for helping," I said as we went back down the stairs.

"Anytime you want to search for treasure, give me a call. I had a blast."

I looked over my shoulder, and Irma had a big grin. "You're an odd one," I said without thinking.

Her grin only grew, and she chuckled. "Yes, I am."

ennifer stopped by after church the next morning, still dressed in her Sunday best. Some people wore jeans to church, and I didn't judge them for it, but I enjoyed seeing her in a flowered dress with white shoes and gloves. Her outfit reminded me of a picture I had somewhere of my mother when she was Jennifer's age.

We sat at my favorite spot near the front windows watching trees bowing in the wind and leaves dancing across the lawn. Fluffy clouds hurried past in the bright blue sky. There had been so few sunny days since I arrived in Serenity Cove, and they seemed extra special to me.

I went into the kitchen, returning with a pot of tea, two teacups, milk and sugar. I poured each of us a cup of lapsang souchong tea.

Jennifer spooned sugar into her cup and brought it up to her lips, hesitating before taking a sip. "That's different."

"It's lapsang souchong, a black tea that's smoke-dried over a pinewood fire," I explained, reciting the information I'd read on the box.

"That explains the smoky smell."

"It's an acquired taste." I stood and reached for her cup. "I'll make you something else."

"No, no," she protested. "If I'm going to work in a tea shop, I need to try all the varieties. Speaking of work, I'm sorry I couldn't start right away the way you wanted me to."

I took a sip of my tea, enjoying the unusual taste. "My first rule is don't say you're sorry unless you've done something to be sorry for. In this case, your father's actions are responsible, not you."

She nodded, and I could tell she was thinking. After a few moments, she said, "Thank you for the job offer and for understanding my situation."

"You're welcome. You'll learn I don't like the word 'sorry' any more than the word 'should.' Sometimes I get the feeling people think they can do whatever they want as long as they say 'sorry.'"

"That's so true," she agreed, staring out the window.

I knew her mind was a million miles away. She was so young to have lived such a difficult life. "Are you saying you might still be able to help out, just not right away?"

She gave me a weak smile. "I'm moving out as soon as I can find a place to live, but I don't know how long it will take. There aren't exactly a lot of rentals in this town."

I tried to recall if I'd ever seen an apartment building on my errands and came up blank. I had an idea, and I quickly went through the pros and cons in my head. The pros won.

"Why don't you rent a room from me?" I suggested. "I have two unused bedrooms, one furnished and one unfurnished, so you can take your pick or, better yet, take over both of them. I have my bedroom and the parlor, so we'll both have our own space. And I never use the upstairs kitchen, so you can take that over if you want. Whether it's for a month or a year, it will start you on your new life." Why should I be the only one to have a new start?

Her eyes widened, but all she said was, "Oh."

I tried to read her expression but failed. Perhaps I overstepped some unseen boundary by offering her a place to live. "You can take your time and think it over."

"How much would rent be?"

I hadn't thought about rent. I didn't need the money but had a feeling Jennifer was the sort of woman who liked to pay her own way. "What do room rentals normally go for?"

We went back and forth, eventually coming up with a number she was comfortable with, which was more than I wanted to charge her.

She nodded. "And move-in costs?"

I held up one finger at a time as I listed the requirements. "Well, there's the security deposit, the cleaning deposit, first and last month's rent." I gave her a grin. "Just kidding. I don't need any deposits. Pay your rent and we're good."

Jennifer's mouth began to turn up at the corners. "And when could I move in?"

"Whenever you're ready." I waited for her response.

She nodded again, her smile widening. "Tomorrow?"

I felt my smile match hers. "Tomorrow would be fine."

She jumped out of her seat. "I'll go start packing."

"Hold on," I said. "What about your dad? Is he going to make trouble for me? Or you?"

She sat back down and stared at her hands before answering. "He might. He might not talk to me for a while, but he'll get over it. But I'm not sure what he might do to you —maybe badmouth you around town which could hurt your business."

"I'm not worried," I said. "No one in this town likes me anyway." How much more difficult could he make my life?

~

MONDAY FINALLY ARRIVED along with my appointment with the neurosurgeon. During the drive to the doctor's office, my nerves began to betray me. What if I needed surgery? What if the hallucinations didn't go away? They might even get worse.

The doctor called me into his office, and I waited expectantly for the diagnosis.

"I've gone over your MRI," he began, and went over the findings, which agreed with the previous doctor. Then he went on to explain, "The brain is like a map of the body. Due to the location of the cavernous angioma, if it were to do anything at all, it would affect your left arm. Have you had any symptoms involving your arm?"

"My left arm?" This made no sense. "That doesn't sound like it's causing my hallucinations."

"No." He gave me a curious smile. "Hallucinations wouldn't show up on an MRI. You may wish to consider an antipsychotic medication if your hallucinations are interfering with your daily life."

"But they're not," I said. "He's actually been rather helpful."

"He?"

I laughed self-consciously. "Thank you for your time." I gathered my sweater and purse and hurried out of his office to the safety of my car.

During the drive I asked myself what the heck was going on? No one else seemed particularly worried, and the chef hadn't tried to get me to do anything evil. But that might come later, after I'd lost all touch on reality.

"You're not crazy," I told myself. Why worry over nothing?

When I got home, Chef was nowhere to be found, and for a moment I wondered if he had gone forever. Wouldn't that be a good thing? Why did I feel sad at the thought of never seeing him again? Sure, he was haughty and difficult, but I'd become attached to him. I cared about him, and part of me believed he cared about me too. I scolded myself for being silly.

My stomach growled, reminding me I hadn't eaten lunch. I had the makings of a ham and cheese sandwich but was in the mood for something fancier. The chef and his cookbooks would turn me into a gourmet if I wasn't careful. As long as I could still enjoy everyday food like burgers and grilled cheese sandwiches, that would be okay with me.

Retrieving one of his cookbooks, I flipped the pages. I came upon a recipe for a Monte Cristo sandwich and my stomach growled in approval.

I checked the refrigerator, happy to find all the ingredients as if I'd planned to make the recipe all along. After all, it was nothing more than a fancy ham and cheese sandwich.

There was enough ham and cheese for the four sandwiches the recipe called for, but I didn't know if they'd be any good reheated. Besides, my freezer wouldn't arrive for a few more days, and the refrigerator overflowed with containers of soup. After a few moments of indecision, I decided to start with one sandwich and texted Jennifer to see if she'd like to be a taste tester.

I hovered over the skillet, making sure the sandwich didn't burn. A humming sound caught my attention, and I turned to see Chef Toussaint scribbling in a notebook, seemingly oblivious to my presence.

"Hello," I said, surprised to find myself happy to see him. "What song are you humming?"

"How can one not recognize La Vie en Rose?" he huffed.

"Lavvy who?"

"Americans," he huffed.

Irma had told me she'd known Emile when she'd worked

with him in her teens. Forgetting for the moment he wasn't real, I asked him if he remembered her.

"Irma?" He looked off into the distance as if trying to remember. "Petite, dark hair? I recall she was rather young when she worked here. An animated young lady."

Her hair was no longer dark, but everything else fit.

"I called her *ma petit carotte*."

"Carrot?" I asked. "Who calls someone a carrot?"

He laughed. "It was our little joke. At first, she assisted in the kitchen. When my sous chef chopped carrots, she would snatch slices, popping them into her mouth. He had a crush on her and constantly dropped dishes or spilled sauces on the floor. I worried about him each time he picked up a knife."

"And you blamed it on her?" That hardly seemed fair.

He chuckled. "He never dropped a thing unless she was in the kitchen. I suggested to Norma that she could help out front as a hostess. *Ma petite carotte* seemed quite happy with the arrangement, often stopping in the kitchen to show off her new dresses."

CHAPTER 25

I'd just taken my sandwich out of the skillet, when Jennifer arrived with her compact car full of boxes. She picked the furnished bedroom, since her father forbade her to take any furniture or belongings she hadn't bought herself.

"It's better this way," she said. "I don't have to hire movers."

Her upbeat attitude didn't fool me. I knew how much disapproval from your family hurt. My brother refused to speak to me at my mother's funeral, angry he didn't inherit her house. I had bought it for her and kept it in my name for several reasons, including greedy relatives. I felt sad but not surprised the house and money meant more to him than our relationship in spite of the fact that he didn't need the money.

My sandwich was getting cold, but getting Jennifer settled seemed more important. I showed her the two empty rooms. "If there's anything you don't want in your room, you can move it into another room. And feel free to look through the attic to see if there's anything you'd like to use while you're staying here."

"Thank you. I'll check and see if any of the books are valuable too. Or the furniture."

"No rush." I no longer believed the treasure was lying out in the open, but rather something small hidden in the walls. At least Bob had thought so—I was sure of it. Harold must have gotten the information from Bob somehow.

I left Jennifer to start unpacking. Irma stopped by as Jennifer carried her last box up the stairs. "I heard you have a new tenant. Maybe you could turn this place into another Bed and Breakfast."

"And incur the wrath of Sarah?" Sarah might be the only person in Serenity Cove I hadn't ticked off yet. "I think I'll stick to my original game plan. I'm making lunch. Would you care to join us?"

"I suppose so," she said nonchalantly, but her eyes lit up, and I wondered if she'd stopped by at lunchtime on purpose.

Irma took a seat by the bay window, while I called Jennifer downstairs. After she'd washed her hands, she joined me in the kitchen to help. While I made two more sandwiches, I put her to work setting the table and pouring glasses of iced tea. We carried the food and drinks into the front room.

"Is this…" Irma began, leaning forward to breathe in the aroma before finishing her thought. "Is this a Monte Cristo?"

"It is."

She cut a piece and put it in her mouth, slowly chewing. She closed her eyes and sighed. "I remember when I worked here, and Chef Emile made me one of these. It tasted exactly like this."

"It should. I got the recipe from his cookbook. He was quite helpful when it came to the preparation."

Irma gave me a funny look. "He was?"

I laughed awkwardly. "I mean his cookbook, of course. He explained the steps perfectly."

"Chef Emile is long dead," she said. "Don't go getting a crush on him. There are real-live eligible bachelors in town."

Before I could comment on the local men, Jennifer said, "I'm in love with Fitzwilliam Darcy."

Irma furrowed her brow. "Who?"

"You've never heard of Darcy from *Pride and Prejudice?*" When Irma shrugged in response, Jennifer continued. "At least Chef Emile was alive at one time. I'm intrigued by him as well, but my father won't allow me to mention his name. He's convinced his mother ran off with the chef, but it could be a coincidence they left town at the same time."

"You really think so?" Irma asked.

Jennifer stared out the window as she spoke. "Dad doesn't talk about his father, but it wasn't too hard to figure out he was an abusive alcoholic. I don't blame my grandmother for leaving him, but I think he feels hurt she didn't take him with her."

I thought about the anger my brother still held toward me. "Some wounds fester for a long time. No one can hurt you like your own family."

When Jennifer blinked back tears, I chastised myself for being insensitive. She no doubt loved her father, and their estrangement couldn't be easy on her.

Irma reached out and touched her gently on her arm. "He'll come around."

THE AFTERNOON CLOUDS hid the sun and the temperature dropped at least twenty degrees. After lighting the fire and pouring myself a cup of elderberry flower herbal tea, I picked up the book Jennifer had left on the mantel.

"Do you mind if I smudge my room?" Jennifer asked.

"If you what?"

She held out a bundle of dried herbs. "You light them on fire. The smoke from sage cleanses the energy, and lavender is for protection. It smells good, too."

"Sure." It couldn't hurt. "If you have enough, why don't you do the whole upper floor."

She grinned. "I've brought candles too."

"Just don't leave any burning and burn the house down."

Her eyes widened. "Of course not. I haven't burned down any houses in ages."

"What?" I sat up straight before noticing the twinkle in her eye that told me she was joking.

While Jennifer burned her herbs, I started reading *Pride and Prejudice*. Elizabeth Bennett's pride had kept her from seeing the truth right in front of her nose. Was I doing the same? Everyone tried to tell me opening a tearoom was a bad idea. The locals assured me from day one they wouldn't support my business.

My bank account had enough of a balance to get me through several months of negative profits, but why sink more money into a losing proposition? I'd bought the house impulsively, used to being able to trust my instincts, without putting together so much as a business plan. I knew better, so why had I done it?

If I sold the house, I could buy a nice condo in San Francisco. I'd once dreamed of a view of the Golden Gate Bridge and long walks along the waterfront.

Still, in spite of everything, I loved Serenity Cove. I couldn't explain it, and I didn't know why, but I wanted to stay and grow old here.

A banging on the door brought me out of my reverie. I turned to see Sergeant Rawley through the glass. This time, another officer was with him.

I opened the door. "Yes, Sergeant?"

He handed me a piece of paper. "I have a search warrant."

"What?" I couldn't imagine what he'd be looking for in my house. I read the document, which stated they were looking for a diamond and ruby earring. Freddie had said she found one in Bob's pocket after he had been murdered. "Why would the other earring be here? The murderer must have it."

"Exactly," he said, stepping past me.

"You think the murderer hid it here?" One look at his scowling face told me otherwise. "You actually think I killed Bob? And on top of it, you think I'd be stupid enough to keep a stolen earring in my house?"

He headed for the stairs with the other officer following him.

I watched them walk to the second floor and moments later heard footsteps above me that sounded like they'd entered my bedroom. If I had evidence linking me to a murder, my bedroom would be the last place I'd keep it. I'd probably bury it in the backyard or better yet in someone else's backyard. No one who'd read as many murder mysteries as I did would be caught so easily.

Not sure what to do with myself while my home was being searched, I stood in the parlor feeling helpless. The whole situation seemed ludicrous. I rarely drank herbal tea, but I needed to take the edge off.

Chamomile, one of the most ancient medicinal herbs known to mankind, was used to treat all sorts of ailments from hay fever to insomnia. Right now, I was interested in its calming properties. As I put the kettle on to boil, I scooped a spoonful of the dried flowers into the infuser. Chamomile was best brewed with boiling water, so I waited for the teakettle to boil, then poured the hot water into the teapot, inhaling the fragrant steam.

Not sure how long the police would take to search my home, I carried my cup to my seat by the fire. I lost track of time staring into the flames, until the sound of loud footsteps on the stairs startled me. I hadn't seen Sergeant Rawley smile before, and the sight of his grin disturbed me. He held a bag in his hand.

With a sneer, he said, "April May, you're under arrest for the murder of Bob Shimp."

CHAPTER 26

I'd never been put in handcuffs. I'd never ridden in the back of a police car either. It was turning out to be an evening of firsts. Staring through the mesh separating me from Sergeant Rawley, I watched his smug face and gave monosyllabic answers to his questions.

I had questions of my own. "Are these handcuffs necessary?"

"I'm following procedure when arresting murder suspects," he said, as if this was a regular thing for him.

"When are you going to let me call my lawyer?"

"You'll get your call, Ms. May." His mouth turned up slightly at the corners as he failed to suppress a smile. "As soon as I book you."

We pulled up at city hall. Rawley pulled into the parking lot, got out, and opened the car door to let me out. It wasn't easy to maneuver with my arms cuffed behind my back, but I recoiled when he reached for my arm.

"Please don't touch me unless completely necessary," I warned him, asserting what little control I could. He opened his mouth to berate me, but something stopped him. I'd been told I had a glare that could stop anyone in their tracks.

We entered the building, and he escorted me through the empty lobby. I felt an empty pit of despair in my stomach. Struggling to keep calm, I counted my steps and reminded myself to breathe. He led me down the hall through a door with a placard reading 'Police.' A woman jerked to her feet, as if surprised by our arrival, although she must have known we were coming. A nameplate on the desk confirmed her identity. Finally, I would be meeting the infamous gossip, Pauline.

A narrow headband attempted to control her curly, auburn bob, and her glasses hung around her neck on a beaded chain. Her dress and manner made her appear in her sixties, but on closer inspection, her face looked much younger. Two vertical lines between her eyebrows made me think Pauline could use a few gallons of chamomile tea.

She reminded me of a meerkat as she stretched her long, thin neck, while holding a stack of papers limply in her paw-like hands. She stared and blinked at me before stepping around the desk and holding the papers out to Rawley. "I have the reports you requested."

"Not now," he snapped. "Can't you see I'm busy?"

She fluttered back behind her desk and sat down, making the papers into a neat stack before folding her hands on the desk like a schoolgirl.

"I'm booking Ms. May for the murder of Bob Shimp."

Pauline's mouth dropped open slightly before she clamped it shut. She glanced at the phone, and I knew she couldn't wait to start spreading the news. When I caught her gaze, I narrowed my eyes in warning, though I doubted it would keep her from telling everyone I'd been arrested for murder the first chance she got.

As soon as the sergeant allowed, I called my new

defense attorney. He assured me he would have me released as soon as possible. "Murder cases can take some time, so don't be worried. I'll be there in the morning to handle everything."

"Morning? You can't get me released on bail or something tonight?"

"You'll have to go in front of a judge who will determine bail. I'll get the ball rolling, so we can get you home as soon as possible."

I would be spending the night in a jail cell.

Rawley booked me and took all my personal belongings. He led me down another hall, opened a heavy door, and motioned for me to enter. He slammed the door behind me, and I heard the lock click.

The room had a single cot against one wall and a wooden bench on the other. I sat on the cot since it was slightly less uncomfortable. Without my phone or even a magazine to distract me, my hopes began to fade. All the reassuring things I'd told myself since the day Bob's body was found in my freezer seemed naive now. I'd heard some police officers were more concerned with putting someone in jail rather than making sure it was the guilty person. Sergeant Rawley's entire career might depend on solving this murder. Did he care whether I was guilty or innocent?

I calculated the number of bricks on the walls to occupy myself, and then my mind wandered back to Bob's murder. In my head, I listed the clues we'd discovered. Without something to write with, I repeated the clues out loud.

"Someone hit Bob over his head with a shovel," I said quietly to myself. "Then they dragged him into the freezer." When I'd heard the banging noises at the open house, the storeroom door had been closed. Had the murderer closed it when he entered through the back door? He must have. Or she. I needed to stay open minded, although I couldn't picture Irma or Jennifer dragging or carrying a man of Bob's size from the garage to the house.

Kyla might be strong enough. Did she have a reason to kill her ex-husband? Everything I'd heard made me think she wanted him out of her life. I tried to remember Kyla's movements the afternoon of the party, but people came and went all afternoon.

Mark had the strength to move a heavy body, and Mark knew where the key was. Anyone else would have had to hunt for the key. It wasn't hidden, but it wasn't hanging there with a big sign saying "Freezer key" either.

I really, really didn't want to find out that Mark was a murderer, but I was running out of other suspects.

A knock on the door brought me back to the present. The door opened and Freddie entered. A wave of relief washed over me.

"You have fifteen minutes," Rawley growled before closing the door.

Freddie sat on the bench across from me. "He didn't want to let me see you, but I reminded him of your rights. I think he finally relented because I saved him the trouble of getting you dinner." She handed me a tote bag.

Afraid if I talked, I would cry, I opened the bag which held a sandwich, cookies, and an apple along with a thermos and blanket.

"Sorry it's not something better. I was in a rush."

I nodded. "Thanks. For the food and for coming. I've been here only an hour or so, and I'm already going stir crazy." Underneath the blanket I found a copy of *Pride and Prejudice*.

"Jennifer put the book in there. She wanted to put a knife in between the pages, but I talked her out of it."

I laughed in spite of my dire situation. "I've been thinking." I opened the thermos and smiled when I realized it held hot chamomile tea. "I think I've let my pride, or maybe my overconfidence, lead me in the wrong direction. I never gave a thought to whether this town wanted a tearoom."

"This town doesn't know what it wants," she said. "Half of the residents would like to get rid of the other half, and almost no one likes anything new. You should come to a city council meeting sometime. They can't agree on anything."

"They agree they don't like me."

Freddie leaned forward, took my hand, and gave it a reassuring squeeze. "Not true. Pretty much everyone who knows you likes you."

I blinked to keep the tears at bay. "Sergeant Rawley doesn't," I said. "I got the feeling he didn't like me from day one."

"He doesn't like anyone."

"And yet, I'm the only person he's arrested."

She stood and began to pace. "I have to ask you something," she began.

I had a feeling what she had on her mind. "Someone planted the earring in my bedroom. Whether or not you believe I'm guilty, you know I'm not that stupid."

She nodded and sat back down, seeming relieved to hear it from me. "But who put it there? And who tipped off the police?"

I stared at her. The answer seemed so obvious to me. "The murderer."

She nodded in agreement. "Which is why we need to find out who killed Bob."

Before I could reply, Rawley returned. "Time's up, Doc."

"That wasn't fifteen minutes," I protested.

He turned his gaze to me, his narrowed eyes not hiding his anger. "You are being released on your own recognizance. I don't know what strings your lawyer pulled to get you out so quickly, but you'll be going to jail for the rest of your life soon enough."

I put the food, blanket, and book back in the bag, taking deep breaths to keep from crying in relief.

"This will take a while," Rawley said to Freddie.

Freddie smiled at me. "I'll wait for you in the car. I have some calls to make."

After signing a few papers and having my purse and phone returned to me, I stepped out into the cold night air, wishing I'd thought to bring a jacket. Freddie waited in the parking lot with a sweatshirt. She handed it to me, and we got in.

"Am I imagining it, or did Chief Rawley seem relieved that I was released?" I asked.

"If you hadn't been, he would have had to stay all night to guard you or transfer you to county jail, which is about a two-hour drive."

We rode home in silence. The lights were on inside the house, and I knew Jennifer had waited up for me. Freddie followed me inside, where we found Irma and Jennifer huddled by the fire conspiratorially. They looked up when we entered.

"Good, you're here," Irma said. "We were discussing how to create a distraction, so we could break you out of the slammer."

Jennifer giggled. "No, we weren't. We're trying to figure out who murdered Bob."

"That too," Irma agreed.

I went into the kitchen and retrieved a bottle of champagne. No need for it to go to waste. I offered a glass to the others, but Freddie said she wanted to keep a clear head.

Irma grinned. "More for us."

CHAPTER 27

*A*fter one drink, my eyelids began to droop. As much as I wanted to solve Bob's murder, the day had been exhausting and I needed to get some sleep. We said goodnight and I went to bed, tossing and turning for hours, unable to shut off my brain.

The next morning, the doorbell woke me. The bright sun streaming through my window told me I'd overslept. Sliding my feet into slippers, I shuffled downstairs and opened the door to Irma.

"Wake up, Sleepyhead." She handed me a pink box with a Molly's Bakery label. "Apple strudel and bear claws."

"Thanks." As she entered, Jennifer emerged from the kitchen.

Jennifer took her earbuds out of her ears. No wonder she hadn't heard the doorbell. "You're still in pajamas. Go change and I'll make you a cappuccino."

"Yes, ma'am." When I returned to the kitchen, Freddie had arrived. My three new friends huddled around the island nibbling pastries.

Jennifer offered me a mug and I took a seat with the others. "Okay, where do we start?"

Irma frowned. "Who are we kidding? We're not detectives. What expertise do we have?"

I grinned, feeling more confident than I had the night before. "We have the coroner, who happens to be a medical doctor; we have an antiques expert who also has a black belt in karate; and we have you, who must overhear a lot when people don't notice you're around."

"That's true," Irma said. "And what do you bring to the table?"

"You're looking at the best software salesperson in North America. Do you know what sales is? Nothing more than finding out people's secret wishes, wants, and needs and convincing them you're the only one who can solve a problem they didn't even know they had."

"That's a lot of big talk from someone who can't even talk the people in this town into accepting you're opening a tearoom."

She had a point, but I wasn't ready to give up. "These things don't happen overnight."

"We're wasting time," Jennifer said. "Irma made a list of suspects last night, and I wrote down all the clues we have. Here." She shoved several sheets of paper my way. "Take a look and see if we missed anything."

Freddie snatched the list of suspects from me and perused it. "You have the mayor on this list. She's still on maternity leave staying with her mother in Seattle."

Irma shrugged. "I wanted to be thorough."

"Irma and the mayor don't get along," Freddie told me, before picking up a pen and scratching off half the names from the list.

"I called all the pawn shops and jewelry stores within a

fifty-mile radius this morning while you were still sleeping," Jennifer said proudly.

"Good thinking," I said. "What did you find out?"

Her smile faded. "Not much. The pawn shops said they couldn't give out any information, but there are two jewelry stores I've worked with who handle vintage pieces. They said a man called and asked about selling a diamond and emerald necklace. They didn't get his name."

We all started talking at once. I took the suspect list from Freddie. "That means Kyla's off the hook. The only man left is..." I didn't want to say his name.

After a moment, Freddie said it for me. "Mark."

The four of us became somber, no one wanting to believe Mark was a murderer.

"He had opportunity," I finally said. "I remember he left the party. He said he was making phone calls, but we only have his word for it. He's the only one besides me who knew where I put the key."

Three sets of eyes stared at me, but it was Irma who spoke. "On a hook where anyone could have seen it."

Jennifer leaned forward. "I know we said Mark had a motive, but his son died five years ago. I know they say revenge is supposed to be stale, but—"

"Cold," Irma corrected. "Revenge is a dish best served cold."

Jennifer waved her hand. "You know what I mean. It seems like a long time to wait to get back at someone."

"But didn't you say Bob recently had his license reinstated?" I asked.

"That's true," Jennifer said, nodding slowly, as if trying her best to make sense of the little information we had.

"He might have wanted to stop Bob before someone else died due to his negligence," I suggested. "Murder is never a solution, but it's almost understandable Mark wouldn't want anyone else to go through the loss of a loved one."

"He was devastated when William died," Jennifer said. "But then, what about the jewelry?"

"What about it?" Irma asked.

"Of course." I got her point. "If Mark had killed Bob, why would he go through his pockets?"

"To make it look like a robbery?"

I considered this theory. "If Mark wanted to make it look like a robbery, wouldn't he have left Bob on the lawn? Why drag him into the freezer?"

"To make sure he was dead," Irma said. "You have to realize, someone who commits murder can't be in their right mind. Not unless they're evil, and I for one don't believe Mark is evil."

I shook my head. I had a nagging sense something didn't add up. Bob's murder almost seemed like two different crimes. A crime of passion when the killer hit him over the head, and a cold-blooded act when they locked him in the freezer.

Freddie tapped her pen against her leg absentmindedly. "I'm having trouble accepting that Mark could kill someone and show no regrets. I think we all are. I mean, he comes here almost every day, helping you fix up the house."

"I don't want to believe it either," I said. "But doing his job like nothing had happened would be the best way to avert suspicion."

"Besides, we've ruled out all the other suspects," Jennifer said.

My frustration began to grow. I got up and put the teakettle on the stove and opened the cabinet door. On a day like this, a basic English breakfast tea would be the obvious choice. I grabbed the canister, and something behind it caught my eye. Jasmine green tea. The obvious choice didn't always turn out to be the right choice.

"It has to be Harold," I muttered as I scooped the loose jasmine tea into the infuser. "Nothing else makes any sense."

"Except it can't be Harold," Freddie said. "He has an airtight alibi."

The teakettle began to simmer, and I pulled it off before it began to boil, since green teas released more bitterness if the water was too hot.

Was there such a thing as an airtight alibi? "I think it's time to poke some holes in his story," I said. "There are three parts to his alibi. The couple in Somerton he showed the house to, the restaurant where he supposedly spent all evening, and then there's the woman he claims he spent the night with."

"Bob was dead before Harold left the restaurant," Freddie said.

"Unless he slipped out of the restaurant, came back here, killed Bob, and then went back."

"I'll check out the restaurant," Freddie said. "They should be open for lunch by the time I get there."

"Can I come with you?" Jennifer asked.

Freddie turned to Irma and me. "I guess that means you're going to talk to the couple. Let me give you their information." She pulled a notepad out of her bag and scribbled down some notes which she handed to me. It said Joe and Peggy Smith and gave their address and phone number. "If anyone asks, you didn't get this from me."

THE SMITHS LIVED IN SOMERTON, twenty miles away, a straight shot once you got on the highway. We took my car, and on the drive, I handed the information to Irma, so she could call the Smiths. Mr. Smith answered and said we were welcome to stop by.

We drove with the radio off, and I began humming, as I often do when a song gets stuck in my head.

"What are you humming?" Irma asked.

"I don't know." I thought for a moment. I couldn't exactly tell her I'd heard the chef in my kitchen who wasn't really there humming it. "I think it's called La Vie en Rose."

She eyed me suspiciously.

"Why? Have you heard it before?"

"Perhaps," was all she said.

Something still bugged me about Bob's murder. "If the killer had left Bob in the back yard after hitting him with the shovel, his odds of getting away with it would have been much better. Everyone would have thought he was mugged by a stranger."

"But according to Freddie, the shovel didn't kill him," Irma said. "He froze to death."

"I wish I knew if the motive was robbery, or if someone hated Bob so much, he wanted him dead." My gut told me the motive was the key to solving the murder.

"Are you sure those are the only two possibilities?"

I glanced over to her as I took the Somerton exit. "You have a third one?"

She paused before answering. "What if Bob knew something? A secret worth killing for. Then again, it could be a combination of motives or something we haven't even thought of yet."

"Are you trying to complicate things on purpose?" I asked.

She sighed. "People are complicated, April. They don't need any help from me."

We pulled up in front of a ranch style home surrounded by neat hedges. Before we got to the front door, an older man I guessed to be in his early seventies opened the door.

"Hello, ladies," he said. "Come on in."

The living room walls were covered in photos and portraits, no doubt of family members. They must have framed and hung all the school pictures and group photos they'd ever been given since they moved in.

"Who is it?" a woman's voice called out from the kitchen.

"It's the two ladies I told you would be stopping by," the man called back. In a soft voice, he told us, "Her memory isn't so good these days."

"How many grandchildren do you have?" I asked Mr. Smith.

"Sixteen," he said proudly as his wife entered the room with a tray of iced tea.

"Seventeen," she corrected.

Mrs. Smith insisted we call her Peggy. I introduced myself and Irma, explaining why we had stopped by to see them.

"But we told the sergeant what we knew," Joe said.

Peggy scoffed. "That man's an idiot." She put the tray on the table and handed drinks to Irma and me.

"Now, Peggy," Joe said in a soothing voice. "That's not very Christian of you."

She stuck her tongue out at him before taking a seat.

"And we talked to that nice reporter on the phone," Peggy added.

"Kyla?" I asked. "She called you?"

"Such a lovely lady." She held out a bowl. "Sugar?"

"No, thanks," I said, impatient to ask my questions. "We'd like to clarify a few things. I understand when you arrived at the house to meet with Harold, he was already waiting for you, is that correct?"

"Yes," Joe said. "He said he'd been there for a while."

Irma asked, "You remember the time you arrived at the house?"

"It was twenty-four minutes after four."

"That's very specific," Irma said. "Did you look at your watch?"

"Don't wear a watch," Joe said. "Peggy don't neither. But Harold did. I remember he said, 'looks like we got here early. It's only 4:24.' Then he pointed at the clock on the mantel."

"And that's what the clock said?"

"Yes'm."

I looked at Irma, and she looked as deflated as I felt. I was about to suggest we leave, when Joe spoke again.

"Funny, though. I didn't think we were early at all. We left here at twenty minutes after, didn't we Peggy?"

"Only takes five minutes to get to the east side of town." She snickered. "Course, at our age, it takes five minutes to get to the car."

Joe smiled and nodded. "But if Mr. Perrino said it was 4:24, he must have been right. Why would he lie?"

"Thank you so much." I gave them a friendly smile and stood to leave. "No need to get up. You've been very helpful."

As soon as we stepped outside, Irma said, "Did Mr. Smith ask, 'Why would he lie?'"

I pulled my keys out of my pocket and unlocked the car. "Sure did."

"Besides needing an alibi for murder, can't think of a single reason, can you?"

"Not a one."

CHAPTER 28

*I*rma and I arrived at the Longhorn Steakhouse and found Freddie and Jennifer in one of the booths. We shared what we'd learned from the Smiths. A waitress stopped by and the three of them ordered sandwiches for a late lunch. For some reason, I had no appetite.

"I knew it had to be Harold, especially after the last time I caught him in my attic. Now that we've poked holes in his alibi, I'm more positive than ever he killed Bob." I looked at their glum faces. "Why aren't you three happier about this? We've caught the murderer."

Freddie grimaced. "It's just that he's a neighbor of ours, you know?"

"I've known him my whole life," Jennifer added. "I thought he was a nice person."

I hadn't considered that. It was probably easier for them to accept I was a murderer—they hardly knew me. To think someone you'd known for years could murder someone would be disturbing to say the least.

"What do you suppose made him snap and murder Bob?" Jennifer asked.

"Greed," I said. There was no other explanation. "He found out Bob had the jewels. Maybe Bob denied it, or fought with him, but the end result was the same. Then he dragged him into the freezer to make sure he didn't wake up later and tell everyone what Harold had done. Harold knew there were more jewels hidden in the house and wanted them for himself."

"I'll call Sergeant Rawley," Freddie said.

Calling the police would normally be the right thing to do, but not this time. "I doubt Rawley is going to take us seriously. A sketchy alibi is hardly proof."

"Then what do you suggest?" Freddie asked.

"We need to confront Harold," I said. "If we can get him to confess—"

"Isn't that dangerous?" Jennifer asked.

I frowned. She had a point. "Every plan has its downside." I wish we had a better plan, but we didn't. "I don't want to put you guys in danger, though."

Freddie grinned. "Four against one. And I know jujitsu. But if you don't feel safe Jennifer, you don't have to come."

Jennifer shook her head. "I won a Karate championship. You're not leaving me behind."

"Does anyone know where he lives?" I asked.

"Yeah, and if he's not at home, he'll be at his office," Freddie said. "How about we pick you up in an hour and go together."

The food arrived, and after grabbing a French fry from Irma's plate, I left them to finish their lunch.

I'D RUN upstairs for a warmer jacket when I heard the front door open and close. It was careless of me not to lock it when I came home. Maybe Irma, Jennifer, and Freddie were early. I came halfway down the steps and stopped on the landing.

Harold Perrino stood in my parlor.

"What are you doing here?" I asked.

"I thought I'd stop by and see how you were doing." He shifted his weight from foot to foot.

"I'm fine, thanks." I debated whether I should confront him or run back upstairs and barricade myself in my room. He didn't appear to have a weapon, and luckily, I didn't keep a shovel inside the house, though he could have a weapon hidden on him.

Chef peered from the kitchen with a concerned look. I didn't blame him. I was concerned too, so I stayed on the stairs ready to dash back upstairs and lock myself in my room if necessary.

"I heard you went to talk to the Smiths," he said.

I wondered how he'd heard that but remembered how fond they seemed of Harold. They must have called him as soon as we'd left. "They're a nice couple, aren't they?"

"Yes." He stared at the floor as if unwilling to make eye contact. "Why did you go talk to them?"

"Your alibi doesn't hold up, Harold." I almost jumped when I felt something brush up against my thigh. It was Whisk. Somehow, I felt better having him next to me, though I didn't expect much help from a cat and a ghost.

"I didn't kill him," Harold said.

"We know about the jewels." My heart beat wildly in my chest. Why I kept talking to him I couldn't say, but I wanted to get the truth out of him. I wanted him to admit what he'd done. "We know you turned back the clock at the house you showed the Smiths. We know you hit Bob over the head with a shovel and stole the jewels he had taken from the house."

"Yes. Yes, I did."

I stared at him unbelieving. Was he confessing?

"I hit him over the head, but I left him there in the back yard. I swear he was alive when I left. I don't know why I did it. He swore we would work together to find the jewels and split the money. But I could tell he'd found something." His voice rose as if reliving the moment and remembering his anger toward the dead man. "He lied to me, and when he turned to walk away, I grabbed the shovel."

"And hit him."

"Yes." Harold blinked back tears. "I figured he'd have a bad headache when he came to, but he wouldn't be able to prove I took the jewels. I found a necklace and an earring in his pockets. I thought I heard a noise, so I ran off."

The doorbell rang, and we both turned to see Sergeant Rawley staring through the glass.

"I'm going to let him in." I pointed at him. "You stay there."

"Can I sit down?"

"Sure. Don't try anything funny."

I let the sergeant in. "Harold has confessed to hitting Bob over the head with a shovel."

"Is that so?" He strode to where Harold sat with his head in his hands. "You killed Bob?"

Harold looked up. "No, I swear I didn't. I knocked him down and left him in the back yard. I didn't drag him into the freezer."

He seemed so sincere. Why would he confess to part of the crime but not all of it? I remembered how surprised he seemed when I told him where I'd found the body.

"But if you didn't put Bob in the freezer, who did?" I asked.

Sergeant Rawley turned to me, his face red. "You leave this to me. I'll decide who I arrest and what the charges are." He pulled Harold out of the chair. "I'm arresting you on suspicion of murder."

I was about done with Sergeant Rawley and his incompetence. "If I'd left it to you, I'd be the one arrested for murder."

"That was the plan," he said.

"Excuse me?" I tried to make sense out of what he was saying.

He pulled out a pair of handcuffs and grabbed Harold's arm. "You don't belong here." Snap went the first cuff on Harold's wrist. "I can make sure your tearoom never opens." Snap went the second cuff. "And if it does open, I can shut it down. Quit while you're ahead." For a moment, I found myself annoyed Harold didn't have to be cuffed with his arms behind him the way I'd been, but there were more important things to think about at that moment.

I don't know why I didn't keep my mouth closed until he was safely out of the house, but I didn't. "It was you."

He sneered at me. Wasn't he even going to deny it?

"You dragged Bob into the freezer. Maybe you thought he was already dead. I don't know. But he wasn't. You killed him and tried to blame it on me."

He drew a gun and I stopped talking, slowly raising my hands.

"No need to put your hands up, Ms. May," he said. "It's not going to stop me from shooting you."

"In front of Harold?" I don't know why I thought Harold would be on my side.

"I'm sure Harold will support my version of events, when I tell everyone you're a murderer and I had to shoot you in self-defense."

"And if I don't?" Harold asked.

"Then, I will put your fingerprints on the gun, and you can go to jail for two murders. I get rid of two problems in one fell swoop. You couldn't even keep this house off the market for a few days."

"Why didn't you want me to buy this house?" I asked.

The sergeant ignored me. He turned to Harold. "Are you with us or not?"

Before Harold could answer, I asked, "Did you kill Bob just to run me out of town?" I was past caring why he did it, but I hoped if I kept talking, he wouldn't shoot me, at least, not right away.

"I saw Harold hit him with the shovel. I thought he was dead, so why not take advantage of a dead body and use it to incriminate you? You'd have to sell the house to raise the funds for your bail and defense, and we could go ahead with our plans. There would have been a nice bonus for me. I was as surprised as anyone when Dr. Severs said Bob had frozen to death. He was useless anyway. Drank too much and made too many mistakes."

I looked over my shoulder to see if Chef still watched from the safety of the kitchen. "Can't you do something?"

The sergeant tensed. "Who are you talking to?" he demanded.

I ignored him, giving Emile a pleading look.

Chef shook his head. "I can't. But he can." He pointed at Whisk.

The cat's gaze was focused on the ghost, and I could have sworn Whisk nodded. He sauntered over to Sergeant Rawley who continued to stare at the kitchen doorway, no doubt worried someone had heard his confession.

Whisk climbed onto the chair and then hopped onto the table. He shifted his weight from one paw to the other until he let out a howl and pounced, lashing out like a wild animal, claws aimed at the sergeant's face. Rawley screamed and dropped the gun as he tried to tear the cat off of him.

"Get him off. Get him off," he cried out in pain.

I dove for the gun, praying I grabbed it before Harold. Clasping the gun in my hand, I pointed it at Rawley. Harold swung his manacled hands and hit the sergeant on the back of the head. The sergeant howled as he hit the ground.

"Thanks, Harold," I said.

"Don't mention it."

Whisk dashed back upstairs as Freddie burst through the door followed by Irma and Jennifer.

"What the heck is going on here?" Freddie said as she ran over to the sergeant who lay on the floor covering his face with his hands.

I collapsed into a chair. "I sure am glad to see you guys. Although, it would have been even better if you'd shown up a couple of minutes sooner."

"We decided to come straight here after lunch," Jennifer said. "I'm sure glad we did."

"Help me," Rawley cried, still kneeling on the floor.

"What happened to the sergeant?" Irma asked.

"It's just a few scratches." I didn't care if he was in pain. He'd murdered Bob and might have murdered me if it weren't for Whisk. "Turns out, Harold didn't kill Bob. He did hit him over the head with a shovel, so there's that, but it was Sergeant Rawley who dragged him into the walk-in freezer."

"Can't you see I'm bleeding?" Rawley wailed.

"Oh, shut up," I said. "You were going to shoot me."

"No, I wasn't," he said. "I was arresting Harold—"

Harold smacked him on the back of the head again, though not as hard this time. "I believe the lady said to shut up."

"I'll get some paper towels or something before he stains your floors," Irma said, heading for the kitchen.

Chef smiled and gave me a thumbs up. "I recommend fresh lemon juice for those cuts."

I laughed as Irma returned.

"Here you go, Loser." She tossed a stack of paper napkins at him. "Clean up your mess."

CHAPTER 29

*W*ith Sergeant Rawley no longer interfering, I soon had all the permits and licenses I needed except one: The seller's permit. Pauline told me it should be approved any day now and asked me to please quit calling.

"I'll let you know when it's ready, I promise." She must have felt bad since one of her bosses was responsible for the delay. Her other boss, the mayor, was still on maternity leave.

I'd put the kettle on the stove when a delivery truck pulled into my driveway. Finally! My new walk-in freezer.

I watched a burly delivery man step down from the passenger side and walk toward the door. The driver, tall and thin wearing a sleeveless t-shirt showing off the muscles he didn't have, stood by the truck. They followed me around the back of the house, and I showed them where to install it.

"Where do you want us to put the old one?" the driver asked.

"You're taking it with you," I explained. "I arranged it when I bought the new one."

"Oh no," the other one said. "Our orders are to install the

new one. They didn't say nothin' about haulin' one to the dump."

A few phone calls got things straightened out, and the men appeared happier about the extra work when I handed them each a couple of twenties. It seemed like a small price to pay if it meant my brand new, expensive freezer didn't get dropped down the back steps.

I finished making my pot of tea and whipped up a batch of scones. I'd started the clotted cream two nights before and wanted to test the result. The technique involved leaving the cream in a warm oven all day or all night, followed by several hours in the fridge. If the results were satisfactory, I'd have to make sure to keep a watch on my supply, since it took at least twenty-four hours to make. I hadn't found a reliable supplier for either clotted or Devonshire cream.

I pulled the pan of cream out of the refrigerator and skimmed the thick cream off the top, leaving a thin, white liquid behind. The clotted cream seemed too thick, so I mixed some of the leftover liquid into it until the consistency seemed about right. Not able to wait, I took a taste. It was perfect. I could hardly wait to try it on warm scones.

With the tray of scones in the oven, I gave the big pot of soup another stir. Strawberry tartlets sat on the counter ready for a dollop of fresh whipped cream next to tea sandwiches covered in plastic wrap. I'd sent Jennifer out to run a few last-minute errands. When she returned, I planned to do a test run as if she were my first customer.

I stepped into the tearoom and took a good look around. The crystal chandeliers sparkled overhead, and the room felt bright and fresh, a combination of vintage and new. The Irish dresser, nicely scrubbed, held a charming assortment of teapots, cups, and saucers.

White sheets covered all but one of the tables, a trick my

grandmother had taught me to keep the plates and cups from getting dusty. Everything was ready for opening day—I just needed one last permit and some customers. Knowing I wouldn't be able to depend on the residents of Serenity Cove to be regular customers, I had a press release ready along with ads planned to reach out to the neighboring cities. I'd have a soft opening and follow it with a grand opening a few weeks later.

Mark came down the stairs. "The sound system is working now."

"That's wonderful." Now everything was ready to go. "Would you turn on Vivaldi for me? I've got some scones in the oven if you'd like to stick around and try some."

Before he could respond, Jennifer returned from her errands, taking a deep breath the moment she stepped through the front door. "It smells heavenly in here."

"Welcome to SereniTea," I said. "May I take your coat?"

She cocked her head, then understood she was part of a dress run. "Why yes, thank you." She curtsied and handed me her coat. Underneath, she wore a granny dress from the seventies.

"Make love not war." I gave her the peace sign, and she giggled. I offered her a chair near the window and handed her a menu. She perused it as if she didn't already know it by heart. She'd helped me design it, after all.

"I would like the SereniTea Afternoon Tea, please."

I already knew her favorite type of tea, but I wasn't skipping any steps. "There is a list of all the teas on the back of the menu, separated by levels of caffeine. At the bottom are herbal teas." I pronounced the "h" in herbal the way the English do, for fun.

Flipping the menu over, she pretended to read the selections. "May I have Rose Petal black tea, please?"

"Coming right up."

Turning the fire on under the kettle, I scooped my special rose tea blend into a small, yellow teapot with pink polka dots. While some teas can be brewed with boiling water, this tea benefited from a lower temperature, about 185 degrees Fahrenheit.

After setting the teapot on her table along with a small carafe of ice water, I returned to the kitchen to arrange a tiered tray with sandwiches, scones, cookies, and a tartlet. A voice from the front room told me we had another visitor, and the approaching footsteps told me they'd come to see me.

Irma poked her head in the kitchen, greeting me with, "That looks awfully fancy."

"Better than fancily awful," I replied.

She laughed. "You got me there. What's Jennifer doing sitting in the tearoom?"

"She's my pretend first customer. I want to be ready when the last permit comes through."

A knock on the front door got both our attention, and I hurried to the door as Pauline stepped inside.

"Hello," she said, looking around and admiring the decor. "Oh, hello, Jennifer, I didn't see you there."

That woman needed to wear her glasses on her face instead of around her neck. "What can I do for you, Pauline?"

With a grin, she said, "I have something for you." She held out an official looking envelope. "Your seller's permit."

"Really?" Out of all the permits and licenses required, this was the last one. "This means I can open my tearoom, right? No other hoops to jump through?"

"You can open whenever you want. Right now, if you like."

"Thank you!" I grabbed her in a hug, startling her.

Opening the envelope, I showed the permit to Jennifer, who clapped her hands.

"Oh, dear," I said. "I'm neglecting my first customer." I dashed back to the kitchen. After adding a dollop of whipped cream to the strawberry tartlet, I carried the tray to Jennifer's table.

Mark reappeared on the stairs, and all eyes were on Jennifer, or rather the goodies before her.

"Would anyone like to share?" she asked.

A knock on the back door meant a friend had arrived, and I returned to the kitchen where Freddie waited for me. "I heard the last permit finally came through. Congratulations."

I chuckled, and muttered, "Pauline." She spread news faster than a strong wind spread wildfire.

The front door opened and then slammed shut. Freddie gave me a quizzical look.

I dashed into the tearoom with Freddie right behind. A statuesque blonde in a black pantsuit stood with her hands on her hips. The buttons on her jacket stretched tight over her belly, and I wondered if this was the mayor, recently returned from maternity leave. I'd heard it took time to get your pre-pregnancy body back.

Surveying the room, she looked down her nose at the decor, reserving a special sneer for my collection of Princess Di collectible plates mounted on the wall. Her gaze went from Jennifer, who sat motionless at her table, to Irma, then Freddie, finally resting on me. She lifted her head as if trying to make herself seem even taller.

"What is this?" She spoke in an outraged tone, as if she'd wandered into a brothel.

"It's a tearoom," Irma said sarcastically. "I would have thought you could have figured it out from the sign outside."

"This building is zoned for fine dining. It is meant to be a dinner establishment, not a place for…" she gave a wave of dismissal toward the tiered tray on Jennifer's table, "little sandwiches."

Irma turned to me. "This is Mayor Wanda Gasden."

"Hello, Mayor Gasden. I'm April May." I had a feeling I hadn't just met my new best friend, but I thought I'd be polite anyway.

"I know who you are." She took a few steps closer to me. "I have been waiting for years for this restaurant to reopen. This town needs a high-end steakhouse or perhaps an elegant bistro the sort of place that will entice diners from all over the state. They'll start coming for the day or the weekend, shopping at our stores and—"

"And you can raise rents," Irma interrupted. She leaned over to me, and added, "She owns most of the commercial real estate in town. Not the Mermaid Cafe, thank goodness."

The mayor's eyes narrowed as she turned toward Irma. "You'd better make sure you remember I could get your cafe condemned with one word to the city council."

"I'll take my chances," Irma said. "Besides, I've worked all my life. Maybe it's time for me to retire."

Mayor Gasden's ears reddened, and she returned her focus on me. "No one in town will come to your little tearoom." She spat out the final word.

I took a step closer to her, narrowing the space between us to less than a foot. "I know I spoiled your plans when I bought this house."

"I don't know what you're talking about," she protested.

"You, Sergeant Rawley, and Harold were supposed to get a big kickback from the sale."

She brushed off my accusation with a wave of her hand, like I was a bothersome fly. "I had no idea what they were up to, and I certainly knew nothing about it. Apparently, the investment group who planned to purchase Thornly house had promised them each a generous bonus."

I corrected her. "An illegal kickback."

"I had instructed Harold to find a buyer who would be amenable to opening a fine dining establishment. It would have been in the best interests of our community. I had no intention of personally benefiting, financially or otherwise."

In spite of my reservations, I couldn't prove she'd been involved. "Whatever your motives or intentions, this house is mine now, and I'm opening a tearoom."

"Your failure will go down in the town's history as a cautionary tale for current and future residents," she sneered.

"There isn't a single place for afternoon tea within a hundred miles." I hoped I sounded more confident than I felt. "People will come from miles away as soon as the word gets out."

She huffed. "Then I'll change the street parking to one-hour parking only."

"You can do that?" I asked. Hoping she was bluffing, I turned to Irma, but her shrug didn't seem encouraging. "Then I'll pave the back yard for parking."

"That would require a zoning change. Good luck getting it approved." She smirked, clearly convinced she had won the battle. "Tell you what. When you're ready to throw in the towel, I'll help you find a new buyer. You'll probably be able to get back what you paid for it."

I felt weak in the knees and reached for the nearest chair to steady myself. My whole crazy dream, born from an impulsive, foolish whim had been doomed from the start. Everyone in town tried to tell me so, but I wouldn't listen. I didn't even let a dead body in my freezer persuade me to give up. How stubborn could one person be?

Really, really stubborn. But maybe now it was time to give up--move to San Francisco where I'd be invisible among the millions of people. I could live my life quietly without all the drama and gossip of a small town. I could start over again.

But I didn't want to leave this crazy town and its wacky people. I loved my house, and most of all I loved having friends. Serenity Cove felt like home.

"April?" Mark's voice called out to me, and I turned to see him sitting at one of the tables. He carefully removed the sheet covering the dishes and folded it neatly, placing it on one of the chairs.

Trying to understand what he was doing, I finally found my voice. "Yes, Mark?"

"I'd like afternoon tea for one, please."

I stared as he turned over a teacup, feeling like I'd found myself in an alternate universe. Mark didn't care for tea, and he'd called the food I served "kid's sandwiches" and "biscuits." I couldn't help but smile at his gesture, but one customer wasn't going to make a difference.

Freddie took the seat next to Mark. "Make it tea for two."

"Aw, heck," Irma said. "Three." She joined Mark and Freddie at their table.

Jennifer jumped up from her seat, retrieved menus, and handed them to our first three customers.

The mayor's glare couldn't put a damper on my happiness as I watched Jennifer explaining the offerings and making recommendations.

Pauline tentatively took a few steps into the room, as if planning to join the others.

"This isn't over yet," the mayor huffed. "Pauline, are you coming?"

Pauline looked longingly at the table where Jennifer and my three new friends talked and laughed. She sighed. "Yes, ma'am." She shuffled out the door after the mayor.

I joined Irma, Mark, and Freddie at their table. "There's one part of this mystery we never figured out," I said as I poured myself a cup of tea. "Where is Norma's jewelry hidden?"

Mark grinned. "We could help you tear apart your attic, if you want. I don't have any plans for the rest of the day."

"I'm in," Irma said. "Give me a crowbar, and I'll get to work."

Freddie piped up. "Me, too."

I laughed, enjoying their enthusiasm for destroying my attic. "If the jewels were up there, don't you think we would have found them by now? I've run the metal detector along the walls and the floor, and we went through all the furniture and every drawer in every desk."

Jennifer had a faraway look in her eyes. "Every desk," she mumbled. "Every drawer!" She gasped, her eyes wide. She stood and dashed out of the room, disappearing into the former bedroom I planned to use for private parties.

We took turns giving each other questioning looks, then hurried into the room after her in time to see her opening drawers in the desk Mark had carried downstairs weeks ago.

I turned on a lamp to see what she was doing. "We've already looked through all the drawers, Jennifer. We looked through every drawer in every piece of furniture in the entire house. Twice. We even looked for false bottoms in the drawers."

"Very thorough," Mark said appreciatively.

She shook her head mumbling, "It suddenly came to me. I once read about a desk like this." She stroked all the surfaces until her hand stopped on a spot under a drawer. She froze, barely breathing. "I think I've got it."

She pressed a spot and a hidden drawer popped open. We all gasped as she stepped back from the desk.

Gesturing to me, she said, "You do it."

I stepped forward and reached into the drawer extracting a dazzling necklace encrusted in emeralds and diamonds.

Then I retrieved a pair of enormous emerald earrings encircled in smaller diamonds along with a diamond bracelet.

Jennifer picked up the necklace, admiring it as she held it in her hands. She turned to me and grinned. "Here, put this on."

I shook my head. "No, I couldn't."

"Sure, you can," Irma said.

Jennifer held the necklace out to me, the gems sparkling in the warm light of the lamp. "Here, I'll help you. Turn around."

She clasped it around my neck, and the three women oohed and aahed. I left the room in search of a mirror. A sound drew my attention to the second-floor landing, where Whisk poked his head through the railings. His whiskers twitched, and he gave me a little wink, as if he'd been waiting for me to find the jewels all along.

Admiring myself in the mirror over the sideboard, I caught movement in the kitchen. Chef Emile Toussaint leaned over the island, writing. Perhaps he had decided to write *Even More Modern French Cooking.*

He glanced at me and smiled. "They look stunning on you. Almost as beautiful as they did on Norma."

A cold wind rushed through the kitchen as if someone had left a door open. I felt goosebumps, the way I had the first day I stood in the room.

"I don't think Norma agrees," I said.

Irma slipped into the kitchen. "Who are you talking to?"

"No one." I replied. "No one at all, my little carrot."

Irma's jaw dropped. "What did you just call me?"

THE END

～

If you'd like to learn more about what really happened between Norma and Irma (and who gets to keep Norma's jewels), order Book 2 now: Tea is for Toxin at https://geni.us/htr2

Read on for recipes!

RECIPES

SERENI-TEA SCONES

Yield: 10-16 scones depending on size

INGREDIENTS:

- 3 cups flour
- 1 Tablespoon baking powder
- 1 teaspoon salt
- 2 Tablespoons sugar
- 1 1/2 cups cream (I use heavy cream)

INSTRUCTIONS:

1. Preheat oven to 425 degrees.
2. In a medium to large bowl, mix dry ingredients (flour, baking powder, salt, and sugar).

3. Add 1 ¼ cups cream slowly while stirring until all the flour mixture is incorporated into the dough.
4. Roll or pat dough until it's about ¾ inch thick.
5. Cut round scones with a 2- to 3-inch cutter or glass.
6. Place scones on parchment-lined or non-stick cookie sheet.
7. Brush tops of scones with cream or milk (optional).
8. Bake for 10-12 minutes until they are golden brown on the edges.

April's notes: You can substitute canned coconut cream for a vegan treat. Also, when cutting out the scones, don't twist the cutter or glass. Doing so seals the edges, and they won't rise as high!

EASY CLOTTED CREAM

Start 24 hours ahead

INGREDIENTS:

One pint (or similar amount) heavy cream – not *ultra*-pasteurized (pasteurized is fine)

INSTRUCTIONS:

Place heavy cream in a shallow baking pan in the oven at 170 degrees Fahrenheit for 12 hours. Remove and place in refrigerator for 12 hours. Skim off thick cream from the top and stir until creamy. This will leave a little thin liquid which you can mix into the clotted cream if it's too thick.

GOUGÉRES (SAVORY FRENCH CHEESE PUFFS)

INGREDIENTS:

- ½ cup unsalted butter
- ½ cup milk
- ½ cup water
- ½ teaspoon salt
- ¼ teaspoon pepper
- 1 cup flour
- 4 eggs
- 6 ounces grated Gruyere cheese

INSTRUCTIONS:

1. Preheat oven to 425 degrees F. Line two large baking sheets with parchment paper. (Have mixing bowl and mixer ready for step 3).
2. In a medium saucepan, bring butter, milk, water, salt, and pepper to a boil over medium-high heat. Reduce heat to medium-low and add all the flour at once. Stir for 2-3 minutes until the mixture forms a ball.
3. Place the dough in a mixing bowl and beat on low for about 1 minute until it is warm to the touch.
4. Add the eggs one at a time, mixing at medium speed. Beat well after each one until fully mixed.

5. Add cheese and mix about 1 minute or until completely combined.
6. Transfer dough to pastry bag with large round piping tip (or cut a corner in a plastic sandwich bag) and pipe 1-2 Tablespoons of dough into round balls.
7. Bake for 10 minutes at 425 degrees F, then lower to 350 and bake 5-10 minutes more until golden brown. Serve warm or room temperature.

April's note: You can substitute Swiss or Parmesan cheese for the Gruyere.

EMILE'S CREPES (FRENCH-STYLE PANCAKES)

INGREDIENTS:

- 3 Tablespoons unsalted butter plus additional 3-4 Tablespoons for the pan
- 1 cup all-purpose flour
- 1 Tablespoon granulated white sugar
- pinch of salt
- ¾ cup whole milk
- ½ cup water
- 2 large eggs
- 1 ½ teaspoons vanilla extract

Optional: strawberries, chocolate, powdered sugar, whipped cream or other toppings

INSTRUCTIONS:

1. Melt 3 Tablespoons butter and let cool slightly.
2. Add the cooled, melted butter with the other ingredients (flour, sugar, salt, milk, water, eggs, and vanilla).
3. Mix using blender, food processor, or whisk until the mixture is smooth and all lumps are gone.
4. Cover batter tightly and put in refrigerator for at least 30 minutes to rest as Emile Toussaint suggests (up to one day).
5. Melt some of the remaining butter in your crepe pan or skillet over medium heat (but don't let the butter burn). Be patient and wait until the skillet is hot before proceeding.
6. Pour about 3 Tablespoons of batter into the center of the pan, tilting the pan so the batter covers as much area as possible.
7. Cook for 1-2 minutes, then flip. (Emile isn't watching, so I won't tell if you use a spatula!)
8. Cook the other side for 30 seconds or so and transfer to a large plate.
9. Repeat with remaining batter adding additional butter to pan as needed.
10. Fill with sliced strawberries, melted chocolate, or other yummy filling and dust with powdered sugar or garnish with whipped cream if desired.

April's note: You'll know the skillet is the right temperature when a water droplet dances across the surface of the hot pan. If it just sits there, your pan isn't hot enough. (You'll know it's too hot when the butter burns!).

POTATO AND LEEK SOUP (POTAGE PARMENTIER)

Yield: 1-2 servings
(April's Quick and Easy Version)

INGREDIENTS:

- 1 Tablespoon butter
- 2 cloves garlic (more or less depending on how much you love/don't love garlic)
- 1 cup thinly sliced leeks, white and light green parts (1-2 leeks)
- 1 cup peeled and evenly diced potatoes (any kind, but I like Yukon Gold)
- ½ quart (2 cups) chicken or vegetable broth (not low sodium unless you must)
- 2 bay leaves
- 2-3 sprigs fresh thyme
- pinch of pepper (optional)
- ¼-½ cup heavy cream

Optional: finely chopped chives for garnishing

INSTRUCTIONS:

1. Melt butter over medium-low heat in medium to large saucepan.
2. Add garlic and sauté for about 2 minutes.
3. Add leeks and cook, stirring regularly for about 10 minutes until soft and wilted.

4. Add potatoes, broth, bay leaves, thyme sprigs and pepper (loose thyme or other herbs will leave black specs in your soup). Turn heat to medium-high and bring to a boil.

5. Cover, turn heat down to medium-low, and simmer for 15 minutes until potatoes are soft and break apart when you fork them.

6. Take out the bay leaves and thyme sprigs, then puree the soup with a hand-held immersion blender (or use a standard blender carefully, processing in batches and returning to pot).

7. Add heavy cream to soup and bring to a simmer.

8. Add salt to taste.

9. Garnish with chives (optional).

April's notes: Recipe has been adapted for one to two persons, but you can double the recipe and invite friends over or have leftovers. You can even freeze this soup without cream (add the cream when you reheat it).

MONTE CRISTO SANDWICH

Yield one sandwich

INGREDIENTS:

- 1 egg
- 1 Tablespoon milk
- 1 Tablespoon butter
- 2 slices white bread (French or brioche bread preferred)

- 1 Tablespoon mayonnaise (approximate amount)
- 2-3 slices ham
- 1 slice Swiss cheese
- powdered sugar for dusting
- preserves, jam, or jelly

INSTRUCTIONS:

1. Beat egg and milk in medium bowl (wide enough for a piece of bread to fit) or pie pan.
2. Melt butter in skillet over medium-low heat (should sizzle but not burn).
3. Spread mayonnaise on one side of each bread slice.
4. Dip once slice of bread (the side without mayo) in egg mixture and place eggy-side-down in skillet.
5. Layer ham and cheese on bread in skillet.
6. Dip the second piece of bread in the egg mixture and put on sandwich eggy-side-up.
7. After 3-4 minutes when bottom is lightly browned, flip sandwich.
8. After 3-4 minutes more, remove sandwich, dust lightly with powdered sugar, and serve with a side of your favorite jam, jelly, or preserves.

April's notes: This sandwich can also be made with ham and turkey. You can also substitute provolone for the Swiss if you prefer. Can also be made in a George Forman™ or another countertop grill. Cook for about 5 minutes for a perfect sandwich.

MINI VICTORIAN SPONGE CAKES

Yield: 12 mini cakes

INGREDIENTS:

For the cakes:

- 1 cup sifted all-purpose flour
- 2 teaspoons baking powder
- ¼ teaspoon salt
- 1 cup unsalted butter, room temperature
- 1 cup granulated white sugar
- 1 teaspoon vanilla extract
- 3 large eggs

For the filling:

- ¾ cup heavy cream
- 6 Tablespoons raspberry jam
- powdered (icing) sugar (about ¼ cup should do)

INSTRUCTIONS:

1. Preheat oven to 350 degrees Fahrenheit.
2. Lightly grease a 12-hole cake or cheesecake tray (or use a muffin tin—but only fill 10 of the cups since they're wider).
3. Cream butter and sugar in large mixing bowl until smooth.
4. Gradually beat in eggs until creamy and add in vanilla.
5. Fold in the flour.

6. Pour the batter in the cake molds or muffin tins and bake for 15-18 minutes until they are golden and springy to the touch. Use a toothpick to check for doneness.
7. While cakes cool, whip the heavy cream until stiff peaks form.
8. Slice each cake horizontally. Cover the bottom half with a spoonful of jam and top with whipped cream (or pipe it for a nice presentation). Put the top half on and dust with powdered sugar.

April's note: If you're not serving right away, stabilize the whipped cream by adding 2-3 Tablespoons of powdered sugar, cornstarch, or dried milk halfway through the whipping process.

∽

APRIL'S SHORTBREAD

Makes 16 shortbread bars

INGREDIENTS:

- 1 cup unsalted butter, room temperature
- ½ cup sugar
- 2 cups flour

INSTRUCTIONS:

1. Preheat oven to 325 degrees Fahrenheit.
2. Cream butter and sugar until light and fluffy.

3. Gradually beat in flour.
4. Press into an ungreased 9-inch square baking pan or 9-inch pie plate. Prick with fork.
5. Bake until light brown, about 30-35 minutes. Cut into squares or wedges while still warm and cool on a wire rack.

April's note: These will keep in an airtight container… who am I kidding? They'll be gone in a day!

What's better than a piece of shortbread and a cup of tea?

Thank you for reading Tea is for Trouble, a Haunted Tearoom Mystery!
Get a printable PDF file of all the recipes shown here by signing up for my newsletter at: https://www.subscribepage.com/htr1

What's next for April May?

TEA IS FOR TOXIN

A HAUNTED TEAROOM COZY MYSTERY #2

Publish date September 8, 2021. Click here to order: https://geni.us/htr2.

April May is beginning to think everyone in Serenity Cove has dark secrets. Why else would they be so upset about Kyla's plans to publish a "tell-all" book?

But she never thought anyone would go so far as murder to keep the truth from being revealed!

Was Norma really murdered years earlier? Is the mayor an embezzler? And what could sweet, young Jennifer possibly be hiding?

For information about current and future books including the Bridal Shop Cozy Mysteries, visit me at https://karensuewalker.com.

Printed in Great Britain
by Amazon

31308681R00128